Thug Holiday 4: Labor Day Edition

Written by:
Twyla T.
Patrice Balark
Dani Littlepage
J. Dominique

Thug Holiday 4: Labor Day Edition

Chapter 1

"Keep yo eyes closed, Stasia," D' Mani demanded as he ushered her along. Anastasia stopped dead in her tracks and sucked her teeth.

"Nigga, you got your hands over them anyway," she told him sarcastically, causing him to chuckle.

"Stop gettin smart, Ma, 'fore I give you this act right out here," he said close to her ear, as he pressed himself into her from behind. Anastasia knew he would do just that, too; no matter where they were, and a part of her hoped he would. They'd been back from their trip for a week, and she was still in her glow. It was like they'd been on their own honeymoon, and she still couldn't get enough of him.

"I already know what you thinkin' and we ain't even here for that." He laughed again, sensing her freaky thoughts.

"Then stop playin' and show me this big surprise already," she whined, rolling her covered eyes. Anastasia ignored the small grunt he let out and continued to let him lead her forward.

"Ayite, it's just a lil bit farther, watch this step," he coached, helping her along.

Anastasia was more than ready to see whatever it was so she could enjoy the time she had left with him before Kyler got out of school. Whenever, he was around, he made sure to sit right up under them. Which told her that he liked D'Mani and enjoyed his company, something that she really couldn't say about his late father.

D'Mani briefly paused their ascent and she heard keys jingling. Anastasia wondered if he had bought her another car that could top the 2018 Range Rover he'd just surprised her with the day of their return. Just as soon as the thought crossed her mind, he removed his hands from her eyes.

"Are you kiddin me right now?" she asked, taking in the sight of a grand foyer, with a wrought iron, double staircase. She turned around to face him with her mouth hung open in shock, while D'Mani's fine ass stood back, leaning up against the tallest doors she'd ever seen. That was way more than what she was expecting.

"This all you, baby. Gone check it out," he said, giving her a lazy grin. Instead of running off to do what he'd said, she jumped into his arms and kissed him all over his face. He had been hinting at moving into something bigger, but that was beyond anything she had imagined. Without even having to look, she could tell that the house was massive and over extravagant.

"Damn girl, all this and you ain't even seen shit but the entryway. I can't wait til yo ass see the whole thing," D'Mani teased, setting her back onto her feet.

"Shut up!" She playfully slapped his arm. "Thank you though, baby; this is…." She didn't even have words to describe it.

"This is ours." He brushed a hand down her cheek.

"Now come on, man. I can see yo ass gone be sittin in this same spot all day if I let you."

Pulling her into his arms D'Mani gave her a tour of the six-bathroom, seven-bedroom mansion. Each room was better and bigger than the last and the master bedroom alone was the same square footage as the entire second level of her house with

Richard. The entire back wall was glass and right next to it was two walk-in closets that were as big as a guest room. To the side there was double glass doors that led into a huge bathroom with his and her sinks, a shower stall that could fit five people with six heads, and a big ass whirlpool tub.

Downstairs, the kitchen was big as hell with a lot of windows that let in all types of sunshine. There were granite counter tops and all stainless steel, state of the art appliances. They even had a pool in the backyard, that had a water fall at its center and a winding slide along the side with a basketball court just beyond that.

By the time they made it back to the living room Anastasia was more in love than before. She was more than ready to go home and pack right then. Without a doubt, she knew Kyler was going to be excited once he saw their new home.

"So, we bouta bless all these rooms or nah?" D'Mani asked, giving her ass a squeeze.

"We don't got enough time to do *all* these rooms in here, but I can hit you with a quickie before we gotta go get Kyler."

"Bet. Come up out them jeans."

The look on his face had Anastasia's body hot. It was crazy how just one look from D'Mani would have her ready to come on herself. Not even fazed about standing in the living room with the windows bare, she took off the leather jacket she'd been wearing and unsnapped her high-waist Gucci jeans.

"Nah, keep them on." He stopped her when she went to remove her heels. Anastasia looked back with a sexy smirk and slowly pushed her jeans down, never taking her eyes off of him. Coming up behind her still bent body, D'Mani dropped to his knees. He snaked his tongue between her bottom lips and sucked her clit into his mouth, making her moan loudly. Anastasia grinded into his face as he added more pressure. Her first orgasm ripped through her body and she almost fell over, weak from the tongue lashing. D'Mani held her up and licked her clean before standing to his feet.

"You be talkin all that shit and can't even hang," he joked while she tried to recover.

She didn't know how, but he had mastered her body so well that he could make her cum in seconds. He didn't even wait for a response knowing that even tongue tied, she would have some smart shit to say.

"Ahhh fuuuck, D'Mani wait," she cried out when he thrust himself inside of her tight opening.

"Ain't no wait, we pressed for time, right?" he grunted, trying hard not to release the moan he felt, about to come out from how wet she was. Without missing a beat, he dipped down and hit her with the left stroke.

"Mmm, yessss, baby," Anastasia whimpered, matching his rhythm as she felt herself on the verge of another orgasm.

"Fuck, Stasia! Come on yo dick, Ma," D'Mani ordered, speeding up his pace.

As if her body was under his control, her muscles tightened and convulsed around him. She came hard screaming his name, and D'Mani soon followed suit, and barely pulled out in time. They both stayed stuck in the same position as they caught their breaths and busted out laughing.

"That wasn't quick, nigga," Anastasia said and snatched up her purse from where she'd dropped it when they came in and pulled out her feminine wipes. She handed D'Mani a couple and pulled some out to clean herself.

"That was the best I could do." He shrugged and buckled his jeans back up, done wiping the evidence of their session off. Anastasia rolled her eyes, knowing without looking at the time that she was at least ten minutes late to pick up Kyler. As if on cue, her phone rang with a call from the school. She gave D'Mani an evil glare and answered quickly, assuring the secretary that she was on her way, as D'Mani tried to make her laugh. She made a mental note to get his ass back later as she hung up and they rushed out to the car.

Anastasia dropped D'Mani off at his house to shower since it was on the way to Kyler's school and sped the rest of the way there. She was glad that his teacher didn't give her any grief because she wasn't in the mood. Plus, she didn't like sitting with sex on her even though she had cleaned herself up. She still wouldn't feel comfortable until she took a shower.

"Where's D'Mani?" Kyler asked as soon as he got inside of her truck.

"He's at home, baby. He'll be over later," she explained, trying not to show that her feelings were a little hurt. He had already told her that it was cool having D'Mani around since they played the same games and both loved basketball, but it was still hard having to share her baby with somebody after having to pick up Richard's slack for so long.

"Okay." He seemed to perk up at the mention of seeing D'Mani later and went back to looking out of his window.

Anastasia thought over what she could cook for dinner on the way home and decided on baked chicken, mashed potatoes and sweet corn since that was the only thing thawed.

Before she knew it, they were pulling into the driveway. She waited while Kyler climbed out and walked with him up the walkway getting ready to call her sisters and let them know about the house when a thick yellow envelope sticking out of her mailbox caught her attention. Without having to read it, she knew that it was the paternity papers. She wasn't in a rush to read what she already knew so she just pulled all of the mail out and let her and Kyler inside.

"Go take off that uniform, baby," she told him absentmindedly as she flipped through the stack of mail.

"Okay!" he said, running off. Not seeing anything worth reading Anastasia decided to open the results, if for nothing else, then to gloat about how wrong everybody was. She scanned the first paragraph and had to lean up against the door for support.

"Oh, hell naw!" she screamed.

It read that Zyree was 99.9 percent Kyler's father! How in the hell had that happened? She had been positive that despite having given her virginity to Zyree that their little sexual experience hadn't been the one to get her pregnant with her son. Besides that, the timeline didn't add up. Or did it? She felt her phone vibrate in her hand and answered seeing the Mississippi area code.

"Hello."

"I told yo ass that was my son woman!" Zyree's voice came through almost busting her damn ear drum.

"Nigga, how did you get my number?" she questioned, not in the mood for the glee that she detected in his voice. His timing was damn sure impeccable, she hadn't even had time to process this shit before he was on her line.

"Shirley gave it to me... so when can I come see him?" he wanted to know like it was nothing that her nosey ass aunty had went and gave him her number.

"I'ma fuck that old bird up," Anastasia grumbled finally pushing herself away from the door.

She couldn't believe that her Aunt had went behind her back like that, but then again yes, she could. It was just like her to do some shit like that, she was the first one to comment on Kyler's paternity. She couldn't wait to get off the phone with him so she could call her old ass.

"Look, I just got mine and then you called, can you give me a second to let it sink in first?"

"When did you get so damn boujie, girl? You all dramatic and shit like it's such a damn shock. I am the one who popped that cherry, so you had to know it was a possibility," he reasoned.

Like hell. Anastasia thought to herself. She had no idea that there was even remotely a chance that they had conceived together. How was she going to explain this to Kyler? Or to her family?

"I'm not being boujie, and despite you "poppin my cherry", that didn't automatically give you a chance of being my son's father." She frowned.

"Well, I did and I am, so when can I see *our* son?"

"I don't know yet Zyree. I'm gonna need a couple days…"

"Nah, I'ma be there in two days, Anastasia. Work that shit out so I can see my kid, or I'ma just pop up," he warned, hanging up in her ear. Anastasia let out a frustrated groan. Just when she thought that all of the drama was behind her, more shit happened.

Chapter 2

Alyssa was lost in thought as she thought back to her Valentine's day wedding/honeymoon in Jamaica. Although she had her doubts of being a wife when Corey proposed to her, Alyssa was proud to the wife of Corey Washington. She replayed the vows they said to each other as well as the reception turn up in her head. Her special day was nothing short of amazing and, the fact that all of her family was there, made it that much better.

The sound of horns blaring brought Alyssa back to reality, causing her to speed off through the light. She was in route to her job interview that was a half hour away from her condo in Manhattan. Alyssa had entertained thoughts of moving back to Mississippi but decided to stick it out in the big apple for the time being for various reasons. The New York traffic always made the travel longer than it should've been. Taking a few deep breathes, Alyssa was beyond nervous about her interview at the private investigation firm. It reminded her of when she was working for the FBI and how she got suspended because they thought she had something to do with the person they were investigating, which turned out to be Anastasia's boyfriend. It also reminded her of the fight she had with her father when she told him that she was an agent. When Alyssa was searching for jobs, she thought about going back into law enforcement, but decided against it because of how her father felt about the police and the feds. Even though their father was gone, Alyssa wanted to respect her father's wishes from beyond the grave, which was something she should have done when he was alive. Since going back into law was a no go, Alyssa decided that being a private investigator was the next best thing.

Pulling into the parking lot of the building, her phone chimed indicating she had a text. Alyssa grabbed her phone out of the cup holder and checked the message. It was from Corey.

Corey: Hey Bae. I got an interview at noon, but I'll be home right after. Since I didn't see you before you left, Good Luck on yours and I love you.

Lyssa: Good Luck, bae, and I love you, too.

Alyssa put her phone on silent before tossing it in her purse and exiting her Cadillac truck that her husband bought her for Christmas. Locking the doors with the remote, she said a silent prayer that her and Corey did well on their interviews as she made her way inside the building. Alyssa pushed the up button for the elevator and the doors opened instantly. After the short elevator ride to the second floor, the doors opened displaying a well decorated office space with cubicles. Alyssa observed her surroundings as she slowly walked to the receptionist desk.

"Good morning. How may I help you?" the brown skin chick greeted with a smile.

"Good Morning. My name is Alyssa Washington. I have an interview with Mr. Moore at 10:30."

"Just have a seat in the waiting area and I'll let Mr. Moore know you're here."

"Thank you." Alyssa smiled before heading to the waiting area taking a seat.

As she waited, it was so quiet in the office that Alyssa could hear the second-hand ticking on the clock on the wall. Alyssa twiddled her thumbs as the butterflies continued to dance in her stomach. Feeling her phone vibrate in her purse, she was about to quickly check it, but the sound of footsteps stopped her, causing her to look in that direction. The man that was approaching Alyssa made her blink twice because he was looking delicious in the suit he was rocking. He was light skinned, and she could tell by the way he walked that he was a cocky nigga. The waves in his hair were deep, and his goatee was neatly trimmed. Alyssa wanted to put him in the category of a pretty boy, but for some reason, he looked like he had a rough side to him.

"Mrs. Washington?" the light skinned man called her name.

"Yes?"

"I'm Johnathan Moore," he greeted with an extended hand.

"Nice to meet you," Alyssa grabbed his hand as she stood to her feet.

"Same here. You can follow me."

Following behind him, the smell of Mr. Moore's cologne invaded her nostrils. The scent of his cologne smelled so good that she stepped closer to him to smell it one more time. Getting lost in his scent, Alyssa quickly caught her.

"Bitch, you just got married a week ago. Get your shit together."

Mr. Moore allowed her to step into his office first before closing the door behind him and taking a seat behind his desk. Alyssa sat comfortably in the chair while he glanced over her résumé. He acknowledged her degree in communications as well as her short term in the FBI. Alyssa explained why her time as a FBI agent was cut short which was due to personal issues, and Mr. Moore bought her story. After answering the famous question, "Why should I hire you for the job?", Mr. Moore flashed a winning smile at her before he extended his hand to welcome her aboard. Mr. Moore informed her that there were new cases coming in daily and that she would be working a case with him first before she either worked by herself or be paired with a colleague. With no questions on her end, he told her to report to work that upcoming Monday before Alyssa left out of the office with a huge smile on her face.

After stepping off the elevator, she retrieved her keys from her purse, unlocking the car doors. Hopping inside, Alyssa brought the car to life before searching for her cell phone in her purse. When she saw that she had three missed calls, all from Kelly, her bestie, Alyssa knew she'd probably seen the pictures she posted of her wedding on Instagram and Facebook. Placing her earphones in her ear, she called Kelly and waited for her to answer as Alyssa pulled out of the parking lot.

"Bitch! Now, you know me and you got SERIOUS problems! How the fuck you have a whole wedding and didn't invite me? My feelings are hurt, bitch!" Kelly shouted.

"Kels, now you know if I would've known that I was getting married on Valentine's day, I would've told you. I thought I was going on a sister's getaway. Come to find out, they planned a surprise wedding for me. So, you can't fault me for that," Lyssa explained.

"They did a hell of a job because that whole set up was nice as fuck and everyone looked so happy. I'm glad you had fun, boo."

"Thanks, boo."

"Sooo, how does it feel to be a wife, heffa?"

"It feels...different. Marriage is a different ball game than dating. You have to compromise and sacrifice more and it's something you have to work at daily. When you're dating somebody, you have the option to leave when shit ain't working. With marriage, it's not that easy. Nobody wants to get divorced and to keep that from happening, you have to fight until you can't fight no more and I'm willing to do just that."

"Say that shit, sis," Kelly agreed. "Well boo, I got a meeting to go to. Hit me up some time this weekend so we can link up."

"No doubt. Talk to you later."

On her way home, Alyssa stopped at Wendy's to get her and Corey something to eat. Arriving at her condo minutes later, she grabbed everything from the car before locking the car doors and entering the house. Placing the food and drinks on the kitchen counter, Alyssa went to her bedroom where she hung up her purse and changed her clothes. As she made her way to the front, Alyssa grabbed the food and her juice from off the counter carrying it into the living room. Turning on the TV, she flipped to the HGTV channel. She loved the show *Love it or List it*. It made her think about remodeling her condo, but being as though she was married now, Alyssa was ready to start a family, which meant they were probably going to need a bigger place.

Before marriage, Alyssa thought about them having kids every now and then. She thought about the pros and cons of bringing children into the world, and even though there was no such thing as the perfect parent, Alyssa knew in her heart that her and Corey would be great parents. When Corey cheated on her and thought he got another bitch pregnant, that broke Alyssa's heart. The thought of him having a baby with another woman damn near drove Alyssa crazy, but since they tied the knot, having a baby was on the top of her list.

"Aye, baby. I'm home," Corey called out, closing the front door.

"Hey Love. I got you something to eat from Wendy's. Your juice is on the counter."

"Good lookin', bae." He gave her a quick kiss. "Let me go change my clothes real quick."

"Okay."

A few minutes later, Corey came back to the front, grabbed his juice off the counter, and sat down beside her.

"So, how was your interview?" Alyssa asked, moving closer to him.

"I got the job. I'm a permanent sports commentator at ESPN. That means I won't have to travel out of town, which is cool with me. I start on Monday." He smiled.

"Congrats baby! It's a good day for both of us because I got hired today, too. I also start on Monday." She leaned over kissing his lips.

"That's wassup! I'm proud of you. My baby is a private investigator. Check you out."

"Thanks, Love," Alyssa blushed. "You know how we can celebrate our good news?"

"How is that?" He licked his lips seductively.

"By making a baby." She kissed his lips again, but Corey stiffened a little.

"We can do what it takes to make a baby, but actually havin' a baby, I'm cool on that!"

Alyssa's lips were pressed against his neck. Instead of sucking on it, she bit the shit out of him causing him to scream.

"Ahhh shit! What the fuck you do that for?" He jumped up off the couch.

"What the fuck you mean you cool on having a baby? You mean to tell me you don't want kids, Corey?" Alyssa got up from the couch walking over to him.

"Alyssa, we just got married. I just want it to be us for a while before we start bringin' kids into the world. That's all," Corey explained, holding his neck.

"Corey, it's been just us for nearly three years now and whatever you want to do with it being just us, we can still do with a baby." She placed her hands on her hips.

"Look, I'm just not ready right now, aight? So, I guess you're gonna have to get on birth control or somethin'."

"Nigga, you done lost your mind! I'm not getting on shit! I haven't been on birth control throughout our entire relationship and I'm not about to start now!" Alyssa shouted before storming off toward the bedroom.

"I'm gonna have a baby one way or another! Even if I have to raise it myself Corey Washington!" She slammed the door.

Alyssa was furious as she paced the floor in their room. She just knew that her husband would be excited about starting a family, but Corey blew her mind with his response. Even though she was mad at Corey for the way he responded, Alyssa already knew that the way he felt about having kids wasn't going to change anything between them. It wasn't like Corey was going to stop sleeping with her. She knew that sooner or later, she would be pregnant with their first child, and if Corey didn't want to be a part of the child's life, Alyssa would have to raise him or her by herself.

Chapter 3

Alexis stood naked in the doorway of her new three-bedroom condo, sipping on a Fruit Punch Capri Sun. She leaned her thick body against the wooden frame of the door and licked her lips, as she watched J.R. laid back on the bed, eyes closed, releasing light moans. The sight of her man getting head from a thick bitch, made her moist. Lexi thought about the way Shannon had just ate her pussy only minutes ago and knew that she was blessed in giving head from both angles. It was a little after midnight and the trio had been going strong for three hours. Although Lexi was tired as dog shit, she still had one more nut left in her. The sound of her slurping the last drops out of the juice box, caused both Shannon and J.R to glance over in her direction. J.R bit his bottom lip while Shannon motioned with her index finger for her to join them. Not being the one to put up a fight, Lexi strutted over, tossing the empty juice container on the night stand. Shannon went back to work on J.R. while Lexi stood behind her, rubbing her big round black ass. Lexi then reached around the front of Shannon, where she began rubbing her clit. Shannon moaned and rotated her hips, all the while, never missing a beat with J. R's dick. Lexi felt her clit hardening and she knew that it wouldn't be long before she busted, so she sped up the pace. Sexy whispers escaped her mouth as she deep throated all of J. R's nine inches.

"Damn, what the fuck, bae? I'm finna come!" he groaned, causing Lexi to stop just as Shannon was reaching her peak.

"I told you about that bae shit, J.R.," Lexi snapped, getting off the bed.

"What man? Stop taking shit personal, the bitch was sucking my dick and the shit felt good," he explained.

"Felt good my ass. You clearly were enjoying the shit a little too much. Using terms of endearment and shit," Lexi snapped.

"Mannnnn Alexis, shut the fuck up! You always ruining shit," he yelled, getting off the bed and searching for his basketball shorts.

"Look Lexi, it's not even like that," Shannon attempted to explain.

"Girl bye. Get yo shit and bounce... and don't think I'm dumb because if I EVER hear some shit about y'all even speaking to each other after tonight…. I'ma fuck the both of y'all up," Lexi warned.

Shannon moved about the room gathering her items without saying another word. She was an ex-coworker of Lexi when she was stripping at Blue Flame. Her and J.R. ran into Shannon at the bar that night and after about seven shots of Patron, the three of them was having a fuck fest.

"Yo ass always talking that freaky shit but every time we bring a bitch to the crib, you end up putting her out," J.R. said once Shannon was in an Uber headed back to her place.

"No, you are the fucking problem. Stop calling these bitches bae, boo, and baby, when they are sucking yo dick," she replied, walking into the bathroom and cutting on the shower.

"I can't help that the bitches you pick give good head. You want a nigga to lay there and not say shit?" he asked.

"Yes. As a matter of fact, I do. Nigga, don't say shit!" she yelled.

"Aye yo ass psycho for real." He laughed, grabbing a face towel and throwing it over the shower rod.

Lexi stood in front of him with her arm extended. "Bruh, you ain't getting in this shower with me," she informed him.

"Mannnn if you don't move the fuck out my way," he said, pushing her to the side.

"You know what. I'll shower in the other bathroom," she stated, walking out, but J.R. grabbed her by the waist before she could make it far.

"Look baby, I apologize for being a man and moaning when my dick is in a wet warm mouth. That was wrong of me and I should have reacted differently," he said sarcastically.

"Fuck you!" Lexi laughed and yanked away from him.

No matter how hard she tried, she couldn't be mad at him for too long. J.R. held a key to Alexis's heart; a key that she didn't even know existed until she met him.

"Let's get in the shower and go to bed; we got to look at the new spot tomorrow," he continued, pulling her close to him and planting soft kisses on her neck.

Lexi wasn't sure if it was those kisses or the fact that she was the new owner of a strip club in downtown Atlanta, causing her pussy to throb. She still couldn't believe J.R. went and bought her a strip club just so she wouldn't never have to shake her ass again. Lexi was forever grateful for him and low key, she wanted to spend the rest of her life with him.

After showering and denying J.R. access to her pussy while in there, the couple hoped in the bed and before they knew it, they had drifted off to sleep. Alexis woke up the next morning to the sound of her doorbell. She wiped her eyes as they tried to adjust to the sun beaming into her bedroom. She felt J. R's strong arms wrapped around her and hated that she had to get up.

"I'm coming. I'm coming," she yelled out as she walked through the condo to the front door.

"Who is it?" she asked in an agitated tone.

"Bitch, it's me. Open up, hoe," Marcus said from the other end, causing Lexi to chuckle.

She snatched the door back and welcomed her best friend inside her home.

"Girrrlll, where yo clothes at? You always answer the door butt ass naked?" he questioned, frowning up his face as he looked her up and down.

"Look chile, this what you get when you pop up at my shit unannounced. Now, what the fuck you want?" she quizzed as she walked into the bathroom, grabbing her pink robe off the back of the door.

"I was in the neighborhood and…."

"Neighborhood? Marcus ain't shit in my neighborhood but old white people," Lexi cut him off.

"Old RICH white people and honey when the wife is away, the cat comes to play," he replied, sticking out his tongue.

"YASSSSSS BITCH! Who is your latest victim?" Lexi questioned, taking a seat on the couch Indian style, preparing herself for another one of Marcus's stories.

"Well, I call him Mr. Bill," he started.

"Mr. Bill?" Lexi repeated, screwing up her face.

"Yes honey, cause I takes the dick like I'm Monica Lewinsky," he bragged, slapping high-fives with her.

Lexi bent over in laughter, ready to hear the rest of the story.

"Ain't shit that funny. What up Marcus?" J.R. walked in the living room and stated.

"Don't pay this party pooper no mind. I'm listening, best friend," Lexi said, waving J.R. off as he began to make himself a bowl of Trix cereal in the kitchen.

Marcus told a story about this old white doctor he met on *Tinder*. He was married but secretly loved men. Marcus gave details on their sex escapades and the lavish trips and gifts he received on a regular.

"Damn bitch, you lucky. I'm jealous," Lexi pouted.

"So, just fuck that car and club I bought you, huh?" J.R. yelled as he walked out of the kitchen to the front door.

Both Marcus and Lexi laughed at his outburst. They had been so engaged in their own conversation, they forgot that he was listening close by. J.R. returned to the living room with the mail in his hands, he sorted through the letters, tossing Lexi the ones that belonged to her. Lexi scanned through what was mostly bills before stopping on a letter from, New York

University. Her heart began to beat rapidly in her chest as she slowly ripped the letter open.

Dear Alexis Holiday,

Congratulations! The Admissions Committee for the Department of Business Administration at New York University has reviewed your application for the Master degree program. I am pleased to inform you that…….

Lexi didn't need to read any further; she had already seen all she needed to see. She jumped up from the couch and yelled at the top of her lungs. Both J.R. and Marcus stared at her like she had lost her mind but she didn't care, it was a celebration.

"What bitch? The results must be negative." Marcus said, picking up the letter that Lexi tossed on the floor.

He read over it before he too started screaming. The two friends grabbed hands and jumped up and down together.

"Wait. Wait. Wait. What are we happy for? You just said last month how you didn't want to go to graduate school," Marcus stated, bringing the joyous mood down a few notches.

"Yeah, I didn't, but with my father's untimely death, I know graduating from Graduate School is all he wanted for his baby girl. I can't let him down, dead or alive," Lexi replied somberly.

"Well baby, I'm happy for you but this school in New York," J.R. said, reading over the letter himself.

"I knowwwww, but...." The sound of Lexi's phone ringing on the coffee table caused her to pause momentarily.

She looked down and grabbed the phone, she glanced at the picture of her and her estranged best friend, Bre. Her and Bre still wasn't on the best of terms but they talked here and there and it was crazy that she was calling right after receiving good news.

"Bre, guess what...." Lexi beamed into the phone once she answered it.

"Hey Lexi, this is Bre's mom. Bre died in her sleep last night," was all Lexi heard before she collapsed.

Chapter 4

"Girl, is yo ass having two babies or four? You getting bigger by the hour!"

"Shirley... leave my baby alone before I put you out," Victoria fussed.

Drea discreetly flipped Aunt Shirley off and then made her way over to her mom and kissed her.

"Good morning, mom... it smells good in here."

"Go on and sit down. I'll fix you and my grandbabies a plate. I got some bacon, eggs, and pancakes coming right up." Victoria smiled.

"Thanks mom... you know I'm not handicapped though, right?"

"You didn't tell the one-night stand baby daddy that when he made you take a leave from work though," Aunt Shirley chimed in and cackled.

"D'Mari don't tell me what to do... I went ahead and took leave since I'm at the halfway mark and high risk. I still do a little work from home though, thank you very much," Drea advised.

"You just take it easy... we find out what we're having at our next appointment, right?" Victoria asked.

"Yes, if they cooperate." Drea smiled and rubbed her belly.

She was always so happy when her mom talked about her pregnancy and spoke like she was pregnant herself. Their relationship had really gotten better. It was sad that it took tragedy to bring them all closer, but the Holiday Sisters had been getting along great ever since their dad died. Drea had a few reminders about Abraham not being her dad, but she always pushed those thoughts to the back of her mind. As far as she was concerned, he was her dad and no one could tell her any differently. A few of the women at church made a few snide comments, but she shut them down so fast that they missed a couple of Sundays.

"I'm going to the appointment, too," Aunt Shirley said as she sat down at the kitchen table.

"And you gon name them babies after me... we need another lil Shirley running around here," she chided.

"Aunt Shirley you done lost yo da... mind," Drea caught herself.

Although she was grown, she still made it a habit to not cuss in front of her mom.

"I'll say it for you, baby. Shirley, you done lost your damn mind. We ain't naming our babies, Shirley," Victoria said and made Drea bust out laughing.

"I don't know why I even fool with y'all wanna be bougie asses," Shirley griped.

"Because you love us," Drea teased.

"Yeah yeah yeah," Shirley griped.

Drea finished up eating with her mom and aunt. After they were done with the dishes, with the little that Victoria allowed Drea to help out with, they transitioned to the living room. *The Young and The Restless* was about to come on and no matter how religious Victoria was, she rarely missed watching it. If she did miss it, she would record it and watch it later.

"Victor Newman gon live forever ain't he?" Drea yawned.

"Victor gon live forever."

That was the last thing Drea heard Aunt Shirley say before she drifted off to sleep.

"Hmmm..." Drea moaned as D'Mari massaged her clit with his tongue.

"That shit feels sooo good, baby," she continued.

Drea's eyes rolled to the back of her head. She bit her tongue to keep from screaming out loud. Once she came, D'Mari stood up and slid his rock-hard dick into her. They both moaned out in pleasure.

"I've been feenin for this shit... damn, give it to me, baby."

"I gotta take my time... I don't wanna hurt you and my babies," D'Mari whispered to her.

"I'll take the pain," Drea persuaded him and he went deeper.

"You like that?"

"I love it... and I love you!" Drea exclaimed.

"You better... and I love you, too," D'Mari said as he lifted her legs a little higher.

Drea's belly was big as hell and she was glad that he had enough dick to satisfy her without being directly on top of her. D'Mari had been in an accident that turned out to be a dream come true. Drea felt like someone was staring at her so she looked up and saw Aunt Shirley and she jumped.

"Shit... what are you doing Aunt Shirley?"

"Wondering when D'Mari coming back so I can get me a sample of the youngster since he got you screaming like that," Shirley laughed.

"Oh my God!" Drea covered her face and realized that she was dreaming.

"What did I say?" she asked.

"Don't worry bout it... just be glad your mama went to the bathroom and don't get mad when I try nephew." Shirley walked off smiling.

Instead of responding to Aunt Shirley, Drea got up and wobbled home. She was so embarrassed that she didn't know what to do. The only thing that she really hoped was that her mom didn't hear anything. Hell, she hoped Aunt Shirley was putting on, but even if she wasn't, Drea knew that her ass would make a story out of it regardless. Drea's phone rang as soon as she walked in the door and she looked at the screen and saw that it was Felix calling.

"Hey Felix... what a surprise since I'm always calling you. How are you?" Drea laughed.

"I beat you to the punch this time, huh... but I'm great, how are you?" he marveled.

"I'm great as well. So, what do I owe the pleasure of this call?"

"Well, I'm actually in town and was wondering if you'd like to meet up for a late lunch/early dinner?"

"I can always eat." Drea laughed.

"What you got in mind?" she asked.

"What about Georgia Blue? You still like that place?"

"I still love it... what time you wanna meet up?

"In about an hour if you can get away.

"That's fine... I'll see you soon," Drea told him and hung up.

When Drea hung up, she realized that she hadn't spoken to Felix since she called him while in New York when Lexi's ass got arrested. Drea chuckled at the memory because her crazy ass baby sister walked out of jail like she had really been in there eighteen years or some shit. She also remembered that Felix didn't know that she was pregnant. He would definitely know as soon as he laid eyes on her though. *Felix would be a great Godfather,* Drea thought to herself and smiled. Just as she was about to call Hannah, a FaceTime call from D'Mari came through.

"Heeyyy baby daddy!" Drea cooed.

"What's happening, baby mama... what my kids doing?"

"Making me hungry and sleepy all the time." Drea laughed and put the camera on her belly.

"Dammnnn, baby you getti..."

"Say it and Ima slap you through this damn phone," Drea threatened.

"My bad, my bad." D'Mari laughed.

"How bout I had a dream me and you was having sex and woke up to Aunt Shirley standing over me. I was so embarrassed and I know she gon tell every damn body," Drea talked as she went to change into something else.

"That just means you need me to come and give you your fix."

"Shut up, D'Mari... but I do though. I can't wait to see you again," she sadly replied.

"Won't be long, baby... what you doing? You bout to show me that pussy again?"

"No, I'm not... I'm about to go and meet Felix for lunch."

"Oh okay... don't make me have to fuck you and Felix up."

"Boy stop... that's my lawyer friend I told you about. We been knowing each other forever. I actually had the thought of asking him to be the babies Godfather."

"I gotta be around this fool before we ask that. Remember they my babies, too."

"I know I know... don't start." Drea blew him a kiss.

"Aight call me when you get back. You got my dick getting hard getting naked in front of me and shit."

"You so crazy. I love you."

"Love you, too."

"What?"

"I said I love you, too."

"You didn't the first time but okay." Drea kissed his face on the phone and hung up.

That was a small argument that they had a couple of times before. D'Mari always slipped up every now and then, but Drea never failed to correct him. He said he didn't see a difference between "I love you" and "Love you" but Drea did. The fact that he always did what he knew she loved made her love him that much more. Their biggest obstacle was the distance. It was doable for the moment, but Drea knew that she would want and need D'Mari with her all of the time once the babies were born. She had been praying and trying to figure out a solution. God just needed to come through because everything she thought of they could never agree on.

Thirty minutes later, Drea turned in and parked at Georgia Blue. She had thrown on a yellow maternity dress that she had picked up from Kohl's with a blue jean jacket and some flats. Right before she got out, her phone chimed with a text message. It was Felix letting her know that he was inside already and left his name with the hostess. Drea let him know that she was headed inside. The March winds were cutting up something serious and she was glad that she had her box braids put in the week after they made it back from Jamaica. Drea walked in and gave the hostess Felix's name and she followed her to the table. Felix had a big ass kool-aid smile when they locked eyes, but his smile instantly dropped when his eyes landed on her protruding belly. Drea made a mental note of his initial reaction.

"Well, isn't this a big surprise." He smiled again and pulled her in for a hug once they were close.

"I know... I know... I was going to tell you, but figured hey, you're about to see for yourself."

"When are you due?" he asked as he pulled her chair out and helped her in her seat.

"July 10th. But my doctor said most twin pregnancies don't go past thirty-six weeks."

"WOW! Twins... congratulations! So, who's the lucky man? Felix quizzed.

"D'Mari Mitchell." Drea knew that he would remember the name once she said it, so she quickly changed the subject.

"So, what brings you to Mississippi? As much as you hate it here, I didn't think you'd ever set foot on the soil here again.

"I did say that, huh?" Felix laughed and Drea joined in.

"I just felt the need to visit really. The city life is cool… and I never thought I'd say this but breathing in this Mississippi air has really been refreshing," Felix expressed.

"Well, it's good to see you. I know it's hard coming here and your parents aren't around anymore, but home will always be home no matter where you are. Remember that."

The waitress came and took their drink orders. Since Drea already knew what she wanted, she placed her order and Felix followed suit.

"So, any special woman in your life yet? I can't believe someone as successful and handsome as you aren't married yet… Oh my God… I sound like my parents." Drea laughed.

"Yes, you do… but I have my eye on this special woman. I'm just waiting on the perfect moment to make my move. You know I plan everything out."

"Well, don't wait too long. She might get away from you," Drea replied and then took a sip of her sweet tea that the waitress had just sat down in front of her.

They caught up on life, careers and talked about everything under the sun throughout dinner. When the topic of D'Mari came back up, Drea confessed to Felix that she loved him. She could have been wrong, but it looked like she saw a glimmer of sadness in Felix's eyes while she talked about D'Mari. For the rest of the evening, Drea steered the topic away from D'Mari just to be comfortable. Once they were done, Felix gave her the longest hug ever and told her that he planned on staying in contact with her more often just to keep check on her and the babies. Drea smiled, but deep down, something seemed off. She didn't know what it was, but she decided to push her thoughts to the back of her mind because it could have just been her hormones making her think crazy.

Chapter 5

Since finding out that Zyree was in fact Kyler's father, the nigga had been blowing Anastasia's phone up. She'd wanted the results to be a mistake. In fact, she'd called the clinic ready to schedule another test, but they assured her it would be a waste of money since their results were the most accurate she would get. Zyree had been so thirsty, he had tried to catch a flight, two days after they had talked. She was able to convince him to wait, but not for long. Which was why not even a week later, her and D'Mani sat inside of Starbucks waiting on his arrival.

"Stop fidgetin, girl, everything gone be straight," D'Mani assured, her placing a hand on her thigh to stop her leg from bouncing.

Anastasia looked at him and nodded, releasing a deep sigh. She sure hoped that things would be alright. After all of the shit she'd talked to him, she didn't know how Zyree would be feeling towards her. She didn't know what type of a co-parenting relationship they would have, or what type of parent he would be. As far as she knew, Kyler would be his first child, and he wasn't regularly around kids so he didn't have any experience.

"There he go," he said, pointing out Zyree as he stood at the door looking around for her. "Remember I'm right here."

Anastasia took a sip of her caramel macchiato and forced a smile as she stood so that he could see her. She smoothed invisible wrinkles out of the silk, white wrap-around blouse she wore and waved, gaining Zyree's attention. He grinned widely and headed in her direction as she went over what she wanted to say in her head.

"Hey sweet heart, I'm glad you could meet me."

"Sweetheart?" D'Mani scoffed from his seat and it was like Zyree was just noticing him. His eyes widened in surprise, but he quickly got himself together and gave an easy smile.

"Oh, what's up, bro? D'Mani right?"

"Nigga, you know my damn name, sit yo ass down," D'Mani said waving him off. Zyree chuckled, unfazed and turned his attention to Anastasia.

"Fuck he even doin here? We sposed to be talkin bout *our* son."

"Don't worry bout me, nigga. Do what you came for and keep that shit on co-parentin," D'Mani sneered, standing up also.

Anastasia stood frozen. She was caught off guard by how things had started. She knew that she better diffuse the situation before it escalated any further.

"Um." She cleared her throat and put a hand on D'Mani's shoulder.

"I invited him to come along because he's a part of Kyler's life, too," she explained and Zyree's eyes narrowed on D'Mani.

"Can we all please have a seat so that we can discuss this like adults? Y'all got people staring." Anastasia noticed more than a few people around them had tuned into their conversation and had their phones poised and ready to record some fuckery. She tapped D'Mani's arm again before slowly taking her seat, but both men remained standing, staring each other down. D'Mani was the first to follow suit, and Zyree smirked childishly.

Once he finally sat down he started right up.

"So, when can I meet him?"

"Well, technically you already met him Zy-."

"You know damn well what I mean, Anastasia," he sighed cutting her off.

"Aye, this yo second warning, nigga. Watch how the fuck you talk to her," D'Mani growled, leaning forward in his seat.

"I'll say whateva I want, this my mouth and that's my baby mama! This conversation ain't even for you."

Anastasia cringed at being called a "baby mama". The last thing she wanted was to be referred to as somebody's baby mama. The whole meeting was turning into a pissing contest between the two men and she was not there for it. She suddenly wished that she had would have brought Alyssa along instead of D'Mani, because it was way too much testosterone at the table.

"Listen, we're here to talk about Kyler, let's keep it at that, and don't call me yo baby mama, Zy." She gave him a stern look and he raised his hands in surrender.

"Now, I haven't told him about you being his dad yet." Holding up a hand she stopped Zyree from interrupting.

"The only father that he's known just died, Zy, I'm not about to confuse him by telling him that you're really his father. I was thinking that maybe you two could hang out for a while, before we drop that bomb, so that he could get comfortable with you first."

From the look on his face, she knew that he was about to protest, but she wasn't about to fuck with her son's mental state, to appease Zyree's desire to be a father.

"I'm guessing I ain't got a choice then?" he asked with a raised brow.

"I mean he is also your son, so if you have another suggestion, besides blindsiding him with this, then I'll take that into consideration." She shrugged and folded her hands together on top of the table, watching for his reaction.

Honestly, Anastasia didn't want to make things hard for him. As much as she hated to admit it, she saw a lot of Zyree in their son. She knew that it would do him good to have a dad that was interested in the same things he was. However, to go from thinking that your father was dead to finding out that someone else is your father could be confusing to someone Kyler's age. Hell, it had really upset her sister, Drea, and she was a grown ass woman. She made a mental not to call and check on her and the twins, since she hadn't gotten around to it after receiving the test results.

"Fine Anastasia, you know more bout this parentin shit than me. I'm just tryna make up for all this lost time and be in his life." He looked into her eyes sincerely.

"Okay, well how long are you going to be out here this trip? Maybe we can set up something for this weekend," she suggested, already clearing up her and Kyler's schedules.

"Oh, I'ma be here for two weeks. I got some business to take care of out this way," Zyree said, rubbing his hands together with a slick grin. Anastasia tried not to even think about what he meant by that as she nodded.

"What are you doin for work these days?" she asked, now that the tough part was out of the way she hoped to ease the tension with light conversation.

"I got my own distribution business. It's doin real good back home. Shit, I was thinkin bout expandin out this way," he told her, shooting a glance in D'Mani's direction.

"Don't expand too fast, we way more cut throat out here than Mississippi," D'Mani grilled him.

"A nigga like me ain't never backed down from a challenge," Zyree shot back.

It seemed like they were having a side conversation, and that wasn't ever a good thing. Anastasia's eyes bounced back and forth between the two as they sat there mean mugging each other and knew that it was time to cut the meeting short. She couldn't wait to tell her sisters about the damn drama.

"You know what, it seems like we covered everything as far as Kyler is concerned. Let me walk you to your car, Zy," she said, breaking the silence that had fallen over the table and scooting her chair back. That appeared to snap him out of whatever he was thinking and he smiled but didn't take his eyes off D'Mani.

"Yeah, I need to rap to you bout somethin personal anyway." He stood up from his seat and waited while she said a few words to D'Mani.

"I'll be right back," she said, motioning for him to stay.

She didn't need them sharing anymore words; they were already damn near about to throw blows inside the coffee shop. Things would definitely get physical if they were outside and away from witnesses. He looked like he wanted to object, but he just nodded and shot a threatening look at Zyree.

Anastasia knew that D'Mani wasn't the jealous type, so he didn't have any worries watching her walk out with Zyree, but she also knew that he was territorial as fuck, so it was probably taking everything in him to remain seated. She rushed out with Zyree before he changed his mind and came out with her.

"Yo nigga must don't know I'm with the shits, Stasia." Zyree cocked his head and asked as soon as they hit the door.

"Don't start, Zy. That shit in there was totally uncalled for…"

"What I did was uncalled for? That nigga came at me first, you know I don't play them games."

"Yeah, yeah, I know. But, y'all have to get along because you're both in Kyler's life, so all that tough shit needs to go out the window," she lectured, hoping that she was getting through to him. He nodded slowly like he understood.

"Ayite, you got it."

They finally made it to the rental he was driving and he opened the door and paused before getting in.

"I appreciate that, I'll make sure to talk to D'Mani, too. We all need to be on the same accord," she sighed in relief. If Zyree could agree to chill then it shouldn't have been a problem for D'Mani.

"I don't think it's gone matter soon tho anyway." He shrugged, sliding into the driver's seat while a confused look covered her face.

"Why you say that?" She wanted to know with a hand on her hip. He smiled easily showing off his perfect set of thirty-twos as the car purred to life.

"Cause I'm comin for my family." Anastasia blinked rapidly, confused, but before she could even say anything, he was already pulling away. All that time he hadn't mentioned anything about wanting to rekindle their relationship. He'd only showed an interest in Kyler, and now he was talking about a family. Shaking her head, she stared off after his car. It was clear that Zyree was about to shake things up, and not in a good way.

Chapter 6

Since discovering Corey's true feelings about having kid's, things around the house were really tense. Alyssa gave him the silent treatment whenever he was home and she spent most of her time in their bedroom with the door locked. The only time she allowed him in the room was when he needed to get ready for work in the morning. Corey would try to kiss her good-bye before she left for work, but Alyssa left out the house without giving him so much as a wave. She constantly thought of other reasons as to why Corey didn't want kids and every reason was worse than the last. Not wanting to think the worse, Alyssa decided to not give the situation much thought but the nagging feeling in the pit of her stomach was telling her not to ignore her feelings and find out what was really going on with her husband.

After starting her new job that week, Alyssa's tension and frustrations seemed to fade as soon as she stepped off the elevator. The rush of starting a new career had Alyssa ready to dive in head first and the fact that she was working with Mr. Moore on her very first case made things that much better. When

Mr. Moore informed her that their first case was on the lines of infidelity, Alyssa immediately tensed up. Thoughts of Corey cheating replayed in her mind but she got herself together as her boss gave her the rundown about their female client who suspected that her husband was up to no good. They spent a few days following behind their suspect who always had lunch with the same man daily. Alyssa didn't think nothing of it and felt like they were wasting their time on the case but when they spotted their suspect with the same man from his lunch dates fucking behind a dumpster on a deadend street, Alyssa was shocked. By the end of the week, they met with their client revealing to her the evidence they gathered and Alyssa's heart broke as she watched her cry as she looked through the photos. After she thanked them for helping her, their client left the office with the photos they had taken.

Minutes after the client left, Alyssa was still glued to her seat. Being a private investigator wasn't that much different from being an agent. They did stakeout more times than none but they were trying to catch a Kingpin. Not gathering information on a cheating gay husband. Alyssa didn't know if she felt comfortable working on cases like that but what she had realize was that it was part of her job.

"Alyssa, are you okay?" Mr. Moore asked, breaking her trance.

"Mmm hmm. I'm fine," she forced a smile before biting the inside of her cheek.

"I'm sure you probably know this already but you are a terrible liar, Alyssa," he stated.

Alyssa chuckled as she shook her head knowing that Mr. Moore was telling the truth.

"You got me there." She nodded her head. "Are all of cases going to be like this?"

"Let me guess... It pained you to see our client hurt like that?"

"It really did. Don't get me wrong. I know we're not supposed to be emotionally attached to our clients but as a woman, I couldn't help but to feel sorry for her," Alyssa confessed.

"To be honest with you, most of the cases we take our based-on infidelity, but we also work cases in other areas like bounty hunter, child support/custody and corporate investigations just to name a few. Sometimes we help other firms with their cases when they come up empty but most of the time, we work independently. This can be a dangerous job but at the end of the day, we are bringing comfort to the clients that seek our help," Mr. Moore stated.

"But surprisingly, you did extremely well on this case."

"I did?"

"Yes. You were alert, you took notes and the pictures you snapped along with the recordings were clear and accurate. Not once did you look at your phone and you didn't nod off to sleep. You were a professional at all times and I'm very impressed with your work. You're going to be just fine on your own or with a partner," Mr. Moore praised her.

"Thank you, Mr. Moore." Alyssa smiled.

"Please, call me Johnathan." He licked his lips.

Alyssa's panties began to moisten at his gesture and needed to get out of his office.

"Is there anything else we need to discuss, Johnathan?"

"I just need to show you how to fill out the report form. Then, you're free to go."

"Okay."

Lawd, please help me keep my composure and if it's possible, please stop Johnathan from being so damn attractive.

Alyssa's silent prayer helped her get through the last thirty minutes of her day and as soon as Johnathan was finished showing her how to fill out the form, she quickly said good-bye before flying out of his office. She went to her cubicle to get her belongings, waved bye to a few of her co-workers that were entering, then stepped on the elevator. Walking out of the building, Alyssa pulled out her cell phone as she headed to her car. After starting the engine, she called Anastasia. She needed to vent about Corey. Plus, she needed to check in just to make sure things were going good on her end. Alyssa was about to hang up until her sister answered at the last minute.

"What's up, Lyssa? How are the newlyweds doing?"

"It's only about to be one of us left standing because I'm about to kill your brother in law," Alyssa fussed.

"What happened?"

"Corey told me last week that he doesn't want to have kids and it's driving me crazy, Stasia."

"What? Well did he at least tell you why?"

"He said that he wanted it to just be us for a while but I tried to explain to him that a baby wouldn't stop us from doing anything that we wanted to do but he just kept saying he wasn't ready."

"Did y'all ever talk about kids before y'all got married?"

"No. I just assumed that he wanted kids. I mean, what man doesn't want to have kids with his wife? What man doesn't want a son that he can teach how to play sports or a daughter that he can spoil?" Alyssa expressed becoming angry.

"Lyssa, calm down. I can tell that this is frustrating you but the only thing that you can do is talk to Corey and find out why he really feels this way. It has to be another reason besides he's not ready," Stasia explained.

"Do you think Corey is hiding something?"

"Don't jump to conclusions, sis. But, if he is hiding something, somebody better pray for him. You remember what we did to Richard's ass."

The sisters burst into laughter.

"We can't whoop his ass that bad, sis. I still have to look at my baby every day," Alyssa chuckled.

As their conversation went on, Lyssa informed her sister that she got a new job as a private investigator but decided not to tell her about the sexual attraction she had to her boss. Alyssa didn't need or want Stasia cussing her out. By the time they ended their call, Alyssa was pleased to know that things were going good between her, D'Mani and Kyler was doing good. After everything Anastasia had been through while she was with Richard, she was happy that her sister had a real nigga that was all about her and her son.

When Alyssa arrived home, she parked behind Corey's car killing the engine. As she gathered her things, Alyssa's frustration had subsided and she was ready to have an adult conversation about them having kids. She just hoped that Corey would be willing to talk about this situation and not shut it down. Entering the house, Alyssa spotted Corey sitting on the couch. She walked over to him and kissed his cheek before heading to the bedroom to change. Alyssa's mouth hit the floor at the sight of the I'm sorry balloons, shopping and jewelry bags. She walked over to the gifts and before she could look through them, Corey wrapped his arms around her from behind squeezing her tightly.

"What's all this, Corey?" She turned around to face him, looking confused.

"I've been thinkin' long and hard about this situation and after talkin to the guys about us havin' a baby, I realized that I was just bein' an asshole about this whole thing. I was bein' selfish because I know when the baby comes he/she is going to have all of your time and attention. I just wanted to have you all to myself a little while longer before we started our family."

"Aww baby," she cooed. "No matter how many kids we decide to have, I'm still gonna make time for you."

"I know you will, bae. But, on another note, the way D'Mari talks about pregnant pussy got me wantin' to see what it's hittin' on." He grinned.

Alyssa giggled like a school girl at his comment.

"I apologize for the way I acted. Can you forgive me, love?"

"Yes, I forgive you but you still got some making up to do," she smirked

"Say no more."

Corey helped Alyssa out of the jeans, heels and blouse she wearing before laying her on the bed and ripping her panties off. Pulling her to the edge, Corey dropped to his knees then dived into her wetness.

"Fuuucckkk!" Alyssa moaned loudly.

Alyssa bit her lip as she held her legs in the air while Corey continued to feast on her pussy. Minutes later, her legs began to shake as her orgasm began to build. Grinding her pussy against his lips, her juices flooded his face as well as their sheets. Riding the wave of her orgasm, Alyssa's body was good and she was glad that Corey decided to put his selfishness and agreed to start their family. While Corey climbed between her thighs inserting his manhood into her wet box, that nagging feeling in the pit of her stomach was still there. As he filled her insides with his dick, Alyssa decided to ignore the feeling for the moment and enjoy the nine inches of pleasure that Corey was giving her.

Chapter 7

Lexi stood in the long line, awaiting the entrance to Bre's funeral. It was a packed house, mostly classmates from high school and a few of their college buddies flew to Mississippi to pay their respects. The cool March air crept up the black and white stripped pencil skirt she was wearing, causing goosebumps to form on her once smooth skin. Lexi locked arms with Drea as they took a few steps forward, gaining entrance into the church. When Bre's mom called and gave her the news, Lexi was devastated. The fact that her and Bre had fallen out so badly was eating her up inside. At one point, she wanted to kill her ex best friend, yet here she was, with tears in her eyes because she was no longer on Earth.

"You ok?" Drea whispered as they made their way down the aisle to the rose gold marbled casket.

Lexi nodded her head up and down before taking her free hand and wiping away the tears that managed to escape. Mrs. Williams, Bre's mom, originally wanted to have her daughter services held at Lexi's father's church, but unfortunately, there was already a funeral scheduled there on the same day. The closer Lexi got to the front of the church, the more and more she began to break down. She wasn't sure if it was guilt or all the good memories that her and Bre shared growing up. Regardless of the bad times they had as of recently, she was still her friend. Two large pink floral arrangements rested on the side of the casket, while a picture of Bre, in her high school cap and gown, sat to the far right. Everything was beautiful including her. Lexi had been to several funerals before; sometimes the deceased was unrecognizable, but not Bre. She looked as if she was sleeping peacefully in her all white dress. A smile invaded Lexi's face when she noticed her wearing the friendship necklace that they bought each other a few years back. Lexi took her right hand and brought it to her neck, touching her necklace before breaking down.

"It's ok, sister. She's no longer suffering; she's in a better place," Drea recited, trying to find words of encouragement for her grieving sister.

Lexi stood in front of the casket and shook her head as tears flooded her face. It was crazy how short life was. There was no way someone as young, as vibrant, someone filled with so much life should be laying there. Her parents always told her to never question God but at that very moment, she needed answers.

"It's ok, Alexis. How about you sit in the front row with the family?" Mrs. Williams approached Lexi, placing her arms around her before leading her to her seat.

Lexi's feet felt like they were glued to the ground, it took all the strength she had in her to move but somehow, she managed. Once seated, the church filled quickly and about ten minutes later, the service began. Lexi stared at the casket and shook her head during the entire ordeal. It was if her body was there physically but her mind had definitely drifted elsewhere.

"You see this?" Drea nudged her while pointing at the obituary.

Lexi's eyes scanned the layout briefly before noticing exactly what Drea was referring to. Not only did they name Lexi in the obituary, they listed her as a "special friend". At first, she didn't think much of it until she heard her name being called on the microphone.

"Everyone knows that we are God fearing Christians so when my daughter opened up to me about the love of her life, I opened my arms. Not only is my God an awesome God, he is a forgiving God; so, who am I not to forgive her? Alexis Holiday, nobody loved my child the way you did. I know you two shared special moments, moments the world needs to hear about. Can you please come up here and say a few words?" Mrs. Williams babbled.

Alexis turned around in her seat and looked behind her. There had to be another Alexis Holiday in that church because Lexi knew damn well she wasn't talking to her.

"Don't be shy, come on up!" Mrs. Williams smiled while the entire church erupted with cheer.

Lexi was pissed, she was not there to be put on the spot and that was not the time nor place to discuss anything that her and Bre had going on in the past, but if a show is what they wanted, a show is what they would get.

"What are you doing?" Drea grabbed Lexi by the arm as she stood up and headed to the podium.

Without saying any words, she yanked her arm back, fixed the wrinkles that formed in her white silk blouse before stepping to the mic. Once she was in front of the crowd, she tapped the microphone twice before speaking.

"God is good all the time. And all the time..." She paused.

"God is good," the crowd spoke.

"Everyone knows me and Bre have been best friends since like the third grade. Me and this chick has had our ups and downs and as of lately, there has been more down days than anything."

"TAKE YO TIME, BABY!" an older heavyset black woman from the back stood up and yelled, waving her paper fan in the air.

"But, I don't know what the fuck her momma talking about. I ain't no special friend. Me and shorty was not in a relationship, I mean.... It is what it is. If y'all want details, I can tell y'all some shit," Lexi jested.

"LEXI NOOOO!" Drea jumped up as fast as she could considering her big belly.

"Nah sister, I think the congregation wants to hear this shit!" Lexi replied.

"That's ok, sister," Pastor Monte stepped in and said before grabbing the microphone from her.

Lexi grinned before walking down the four steps that led to the seats. She stopped at the casket, leaned down and placed a soft kiss on Bre's cold cheek before raising her index finger in the air and walking down the aisle and out of the church doors with Drea's wobbling ass in tow.

"Alexis, tell me you didn't just do that," an out of breath Drea said once they were inside her car.

"Yes, the fuck I did. I hate them fake ass Christians, sis. Them motherfuckers irk my nerves," Lexi grimaced.

"But Lexi…"

"But Drea…."

"You know what, when you get like this, can't nobody tell you shit," Drea replied, finally pulling away from the curb into traffic.

The ride back to Drea's place was a quiet one. Lexi had a blunt already rolled in her purse but she knew Drea's granny ass would have a fit if she hit the blunt in her ride so she just waited until she got back to the crib. It was about an hour drive back to Jackson and Lexi was thankful that her oldest sister didn't give her one of those lawyer ass lectures during the ride. Once they pulled into Drea's driveway, Lexi grabbed her Birkin bag and got out the car.

"Don't be slamming my damn door!" Drea yelled.

"Fuck you and that raggedy ass door," Lexi yelled back before stepping across the lawn heading to her parents' house.

"Oh, so cuz you mad, you staying with Ma?" Drea quizzed, placing her hands on her hips, but Lexi only gave her the middle finger.

"Ok lil hoe… I bet I tell mommy what you did today in those people's church, too," she barked, walking as fast as she could, trying to beat Lexi to the front door.

"Old fat pregnant snitch ass. You lucky you popped or I would have tripped the shit outta you," Lexi chuckled running to the front door before Drea could.

Once inside, the sisters found their mom and Aunt Shirley at the kitchen table talking.

"How was the services, baby?" Mrs. Holiday asked, hugging Lexi first, followed by Drea.

"It was ummmmm interesting," Drea coughed.

"Interesting, huh? Well one of my home girls is actually friends with ya ex-girlfriend's mother and she told me that...." Shirley began to spill the tea but Lexi interrupted her.

"AUNT SHIRLEY, YOU WANNA SMOKE THIS BLUNT WITH ME!" Lexi yelled out.

"Well, I don't mind if I do," Shirley replied, standing to her feet, heading towards the door, completely dismissing what she was about to say.

Chapter 8

"Oh, my God... aww!" Hannah exclaimed while her hand was on Drea's belly and she felt the babies kicking and moving around.

"It feels so weird, but sooo good. I'm really still in shock," Drea bubbled.

"Well girl, it's real. I can't wait to meet my Godbabies in a few months."

"Wait... who said you the God mommy?" Lexi appeared and asked Hannah.

"Lexi... don't start," Drea laughed at her crazy ass sister.

"Nah, but I'm for real... why I can't be the twin's God mommy?"

"Ummm because you have a title... you're their TT," Hannah replied.

"But two other bitches got that title, too," Lexi pouted.

"Lexxiiii... stop it. We've all been getting along so great, and Hannah's right. You're one of the TT's. We not gonna get caught up on titles."

"I guess, but Ima have the babies call Lyssa and Stasia just that… Lyssa and Stasia," Lexi shrugged.

Drea couldn't do shit but laugh at Lexi. Baby Holiday wasn't ever gonna change and they all knew it and accepted it.

"Lexi you going by Bre parents' house?" Drea quizzed.

"Hell naw… I still can't believe she put me on the spot like that," Lexi fussed.

"She was only going off of what she thought, Lexi. I think you should at least go by and see her before you leave," Drea expressed and Lexi blew her off.

Drea and Hannah talked for a little while longer and then Hannah finally left and went home. Time was ticking by so slow and Drea was becoming impatient. Just as she was about to pick up her phone to call D'Mari, it rang and a selfie that he had taken in Jamaica popped up on the screen along with his customized ringtone.

"I was just about to call you, baby. Where are you?"

"Is that right? Well open the door and you'll see me."

Drea got up so fast that she almost fell. As soon as she opened the door, there stood her man looking fine as ever. Her pussy instantly got wet as she stared at him from head to toe. Even dressed down in a simple polo tee and jeans, he was the type that still would have all eyes on him. D'Mari wasted no time pulling her in for a kiss. Once he broke the kiss, Drea looked down as he made his way to her belly and began kissing and rubbing on it. It was the cutest thing ever and she couldn't help but to smile from ear to ear. Drea was still in awe that she was going to be somebody's mommy soon; actually, two little somebody's. It was surreal, but she couldn't wait.

"I would ask if you fed my babies, but I know you have," D'Mari said after he finally stood up a couple minutes later.

"Oh, you being funny?" Drea sassed.

"Nah baby... I was just... never mind let me just hush," D'Mari kissed her instead of digging a deeper hole for himself.

"Yeah... that's a good idea," Drea playfully hit him upside the head.

Later that night, Drea was content as ever as she was snuggled into D'Mari's tight embrace. She had lost count on how many times he made her cum. They definitely made up for lost time.

"So, what you want? Boys, girls, or a boy and a girl?" D'Mari asked her.

"As long as they are healthy, it really doesn't even matter," Drea expressed.

"But let me guess… you want boys?" she continued.

"Honestly, I feel the same as you, but of course I won't trip if it's boys," he told her.

"You say that now but let us pop up with two girls you gon be mad," Drea teased.

"If that happen then I just gotta knock you right back up to get a son."

"What the hell? You tripping." Drea playfully rolled her eyes.

"Dead ass, you can't be selfish."

"Let me start praying now then… what you think about a fall wedding though? You think it'll be too soon?"

"It's never too soon. We can do it tomorrow if you want."

"Aww babe, you're so sweet. I was thinking Labor Day Weekend? I can't wait to become Mrs. Mitchell." Drea held her hand up and admired her ring.

"Let's do it then," D'Mari agreed.

After another round of sex, they drifted off to sleep both anxiously awaiting the next day.

***

"It seems like we going to the movies instead of a doctor's appointment," Drea laughed as she looked in the side mirror as Lexi was right on D'Mari' ass.

They were on their way to Drea's doctor's appointment with her family following behind. Drea knew why Aunt Shirley hopped in with Lexi, but both of their mouths dropped when Victoria beat Shirley to the front seat. That smoke session was cut short and Drea was too tickled. She knew that they would make up for it later either way it went.

"I was thinkin the same shit, but it's good to have family support like that. I know my moms can't wait to find out what we having so she can start shopping. If it wasn't for her own appointment, she would be here today, too," D'Mari explained.

"She calls every other day. I can't wait to officially meet her," Drea beamed.

They arrived at the clinic about thirty minutes later and D'Mari pulled right in the front of the door and parked. He helped Drea out of the car, walked her inside and then left to go and park the car.

"Wheewww if you ever let that man go, Ima be right here to swoop him up," Aunt Shirley said as soon as she entered the clinic.

"You want everybody man auntie, damn… I mean dang," Lexi said.

"Damn right… and J.R. want me, too; but since you my fav, you ain't got no worries," Aunt Shirley told Lexi.

"Lord Shirley… can you act like you got some sense just for today?" Victoria pleaded.

Drea laughed as her auntie waved her mom off. A few minutes later D'Mari walked back in and took his seat by Drea. When her name was called a few minutes later, she told everyone to stay seated because she knew she was only going to give a urine sample and get her vitals checked. She knew there was no need in them getting up at the moment, but with the way that her doctor operated, the wait wouldn't be long. Drea's blood pressure was fine, but she cringed when she stepped on the scale.

"Don't you dare try to be sad. You're carrying twins and you still look wonderful," the nurse told her and made her smile a little.

She walked back out and saw that Aunt Shirley had hopped in her seat. If it was anyone else, Drea would have cursed them out, but she knew that her aunt was only doing shit to get a reaction. Drea had only been sitting down for two good minutes before her name was called again. D'Mari was right by her side and the rest of the crew followed as the nurse led them to the sonogram room. Everyone got as comfortable as possible. D'Mari stood up while everyone found somewhere to sit.

"Wheewww… we having a family reunion today. How's everybody doing?" Dr. Livingston walked in and chirped.

"Something like that," Drea beamed.

"Well, that's fine by me… everybody excited to find out what we're having I'm sure. Do we wanna know today?"

"Yes… we're all so…"

"They all excited, doc. But, I'm doing a gender reveal so I need for you to put those results in an envelope and give it to me when you're done," Lexi cut Drea off.

"Lexi… really? What you let everybody pile up and come to the appointment for? D'Mari wants to know what we're having," Drea fussed.

"Drea, it's really you…" D'Mari started saying, but Drea gave him the evil eye and shut him up.

"Don't lie on my brother-in-law, yo nosey as… you the one wanna know. Besides, I'll tell him," Lexi rolled her eyes.

"Well, let's get this underway. Everything looked fine from your lab work. Just keep doing what you've been doing," Dr. Livingston said as she raised Drea's shirt and put gel on her belly.

A few moments later the babies' heartbeats resounded in the room and the smiles from everyone could be felt. Dr. Livingston informed them that the babies were weighing one and a half pounds each and let Drea know that everything was on schedule.

"Before I click here, I need everyone to close their eyes," the doctor stated, playing along with Lexi's game.

Drea finally did as she was told, but not before rolling her eyes at Lexi and flipping her off once she saw her mom had her eyes closed.

"Yeesss!!!" Lexi squealed after a few seconds and everyone opened their eyes.

"Lexi, you gon tell me what the babies are, too... I ain't waiting til no gender reveal," Shirley fussed.

"You know I love you, Aunt Shirley, but nope because you got a big mouth. Gender reveal will be the day after my graduation in Atlanta," Lexi informed them.

"That's next month, Lexi," Drea fussed.

"I know... the time will fly by," Lexui winked and walked out of the room with the envelope secure in her hands.

Drea wanted to fuss, but she bit her tongue and let her baby sister have her way.

Chapter 9

Anastasia waited for her sisters to pick up the FaceTime call nervously. She had been dreading having to tell them about the whole "Zyree situation". Especially, after the way she had denied the possibility of him being Kyler's father, but she needed to talk to somebody about his advances. Why not her sisters? At least they would be able to give her some solid advice... after they poked their fun.

"Hey sister!"

"What's up, sis?"

"Hey bitch!"

"Hey Holiday sisters," she said as their faces popped up on her phone.

"Damn Drea, your face getting fat," she noted, taking in how much her sister seemed to have changed since she last saw her.

"I wasn't gone say nothin, but since Stasia brought it up, you are lookin a lil more round in the face, Drea. What yo ass been eatin since vacation?"

"Fuck both y'all, okay?" Drea sniffed and flipped them the bird.

"Leave her alone, y'all; she is eating for three," Lyssa chimed in.

"Right, y'all over there soundin just like Aunt Shirley's worrisome ass, besides my man like it." She stuck out her tongue into the camera causing them all to laugh.

"Okay new topic cause ain't nobody tryna think about D'Mari's pregnancy fetishes.

Anastasia joked before taking a deep breath. "The reason I called y'all is because I got my results back from the paternity test, and Zyree-."

"*Is* the father! Bitch, I told yo ass!" Lexi cut her off yelling.

"Oh, my God! What he say? What D'Mani say? Does Kyler know?" Drea shot out question after question while Alyssa sat with her mouth open and Lexi started twerking.

"Well, Kyler doesn't know yet and D'Mani was cool until we had that meeting with him." Anastasia frowned, irritated by

Lexi doing a whole dance routine like some music was playing, while Alyssa was still shocked silent.

"Y'all met up already?" Lyssa questioned finally speaking.

"Dammit Lexi, stop twerkin in the camera! I can't even concentrate on what I wanna say!"

"Welllll, I'm happy hoe, yo ass never admit when you're wrong about somethin! Wait till I tell Aunt Shirley!"

"She's the whole reason I'm in this mess now, then she went and gave his ass my number so she probably already knows," Anastasia said, rolling her eyes.

"That sound just like Aunt Shirley's messy ass," Alyssa shook her head.

"Yeah, it sure as hell do. I can't wait to see her drunk ass! She better hope I don't replace her liquor with juice and water."

"She gone fuck you up, Stasia! You bet not play with her alcohol," Lexi warned out of breath, when she finally rejoined the conversation and stopped shaking her ass.

"Well, when exactly did you find out and what is Zyree talking about?" Drea asked in her lawyer voice.

After she took another deep breath, Anastasia ran down everything that had happened since the first time Zyree called. Their expressions went from surprise to horrified after hearing the way that he'd been acting. Except for Alexis who seemed to find humor in it all.

"Biiiitch! You better get his ass before bro handle that shit for you." Lexi was the first to speak when Anastasia finished filling them in.

"No, tell D'Mani now before he finds out on his own, Stasia, maybe all y'all can sit down and talk about boundaries."

"Hell naw, Drea! The last time we tried that, their asses was bouta start fightin in fuckin Starbucks!" There was no way Stasia was about to try and have another meeting with both men to address Zyree coming at her. Especially after D'Mani had already warned him. There wouldn't even be a meeting. D'Mani would be at his head as soon as Stasia let the words leave her lips.

"Yeah that's true, but you can't just not tell him, I mean damn what you gone do? It's not like you considering his advances... right?" Alyssa chimed with raised brows.

"Hell, she bet not be, as much shit as she been through to be with D'Mani!" Lexi said, sucking her teeth.

"Exactly, baby Holiday! You took the words right out my mouth."

"Hell no! I ain't considerin anything with that nigga!" Anastasia shuddered.

It wasn't like she didn't find him attractive or anything, but she loved D'Mani, and like her sisters had said, she'd been through a lot to be with him.

"I actually called to get y'all advice, because I don't know what to do." Her sisters all seemed to be thinking hard about the best thing for her to do, but like her, they seemed to be coming up empty.

"How bout this?" Drea finally spoke. "Just continue to reject his advances, and make sure to keep a record of them. Let him know that if he isn't contacting you about Kyler then you don't have anything to talk about," she coached.

"Don't you think I tried that?"

"Well, try harder! I'll be in New York soon, to see D'Mari and I'll have something figured out by then." She shrugged and Stasia had no choice but to accept whatever advice she could at the moment. It beat the hell out of telling D'Mani and risking him kicking Zyree's ass or worse.

"Damn, I wanna watch the drama unfold!" Lexi whined.

"Y'all gone have front row seats while I'm here being bored."

"You just like yo messy ass Aunty, girl." Lyssa shook her head, while Lexi just nodded.

"Of course, she don't call me her favorite for nothin." She shrugged.

"Okay, well I'll talk to y'all later. Give the guys my love and Drea kiss the babies for me," Stasia said, trying to rush off the phone so she could answer the door for whoever was leaning on her bell.

"First of all, I ain't givin my nigga no love from yo friendly ass, and bitch how she gone kiss her own belly?" Lexi smacked.

"Fuck you, heffa, and she can kiss her fingers and put them on her- never mind, I'ma talk to y'all later," she dismissed and ended the call quickly. Anastasia maneuvered around the litter of boxes that crowded the floor since they'd been packing to move to the new house. D'Mani had taken Kyler with him to get more boxes, and duct tape, which thankfully had taken long enough for her to get her call in with her sisters. Lately, they had been damn near joined at the hip and it had already been hard to hide Zyree's activity from him. That nigga was not letting up no matter what she said. She hoped his life wouldn't have to end for him to leave her alone. Once she finally made it to the door, she smoothed her hair out of her face and pulled it open. A deliveryman stood before her holding a large bouquet of red roses, and a gold garment box, with a matching envelope attached.

"Anastasia Holiday?" he asked, smiling and extending the items in her direction.

"Yeah, that's me." She gushed feeling her insides melt at the gesture. D'Mani had really been being extremely romantic as of late. Ever since he'd shown her the house, he'd been surprising her with "just because" gifts, almost every day. She sniffed the roses while the guy got his clipboard and handed her a pen.

"Just sign right there, ma'am." She hurriedly scribbled her name across the bottom of the paper. She was handing back the pen when the sound of D'Mani's angry voice stopped her and sent a chill down her spine.

"What the fuck is this shit?" he questioned, walking up with a bouquet of his own, a small blue bag from Tiffany's and Kyler beside him carrying a heart shaped box of chocolate. The deliveryman wasted no time and got his ass out of there quick since D'Mani's body language screamed pissed. The way D'Mani was looking at her had Anastasia ready to break out into a sprint. It was obvious that D'Mani hadn't been the one to send her the items in her arms and only one other person could come to mind who would have sent them otherwise... *Zyree.*

Oh shit!

"Heeyy baby," Anastasia purred trying to get herself together. Somehow, she managed to slide the envelope underneath the package as she stepped closer to D'Mani as he stared after the deliveryman with a scowl.

"Who sent that shit?" He wanted to know, turning his angry glare on her. D'Mani looked over the array of things in her hands and then back up to her face.

"Oh, this is just something Alyssa sent over. She said it was so that I could romance you," she told him, smiling nervously. Years of lying to Richard had her prepped and ready to go whenever the need arose, but from the way he was scrutinizing her, she wasn't sure if it was working on D'Mani.

"Alyssa sent you flowers and shit, after she just got married?" The way he asked made the lie seem stupid but it was too late for her to back out now.

"Yeah, um you know how we're all trying to repair our relationship. She sent Drea and Lexi some, too." Anastasia tried to control the shaky high pitch that her voice had taken on, knowing that if she didn't relax she would give herself away. D'Mani didn't say anything, he just continued to look her over which made her even more nervous. Feeling her smile start to falter, she looked down at the flowers and bag he was holding.

"What's all this?"

"We brought you presents!" Kyler chirped, happily unaware of the tension.

"I see! You gonna help me eat some of these chocolates?" she asked. He looked up at D'Mani before answering, and shouted out "yeah," when he finally nodded. D'Mani was smiling down at him, but she could tell it was forced.

"Thank you, baby."

Anastasia leaned up and gave him a kiss as she eased the gifts from his hands. It took him a minute, but he eventually returned her affection.

"Let's go put these in some water and see what else y'all brought me." She reached for Kyler with her free hand and they started towards the house with D'Mani following closely behind.

Hours later, after they had finished their packing for the day and dinner, Anastasia lay in bed waiting on D'Mani to get out of the shower. His mood had been off the whole night and she knew it was because he didn't believe her about the flowers and dress. The little black Givenchy dress was beautiful and D'Mani had watched her like a hawk when she'd unwrapped it. If it had come from him it was definitely something that she would have worn, but since it wasn't, she was sending that shit right back. When she went to throw the box away, she read the card attached.

Dear Stasia,

I know it's been a long time, but I'm older and ready to fight for you like I didn't before. We already got a son, now we just need the rings. I hope you'll meet me for dinner this weekend.

Love always

Zyree.

She instantly ripped that shit up wondering why that fool was so hell bent on getting her back when they had only been together once, and it was years ago. She wasn't going to let him ruin what she had with D'Mani; there was no way. Of course, his stalking ass called her damn near every hour on the hour, further making D'Mani give her the silent treatment. It wasn't nothing that a little loving couldn't fix, so after her shower she got ready to put it on him. She had candles lit and soft music playing as she laid in bed naked. When the door to the bathroom opened a thick fog of steam beat D'Mani through the door and she struck a sexy pose. He looked her way briefly and went over to put on a pair of boxers before sliding into bed beside her and turning his back.

"I ain't yo dumb ass ex, Stasia," he said once he was comfortable. "I pay more attention to you, so I know when you lyin. Don't get that nigga killed because he can't take no for an answer." And with that he stopped talking and went to sleep leaving Anastasia shaken and confused.

Chapter 10

With her and Corey fucking like a nigga fresh out of prison, it was hard for Alyssa to drag herself out of bed in the mornings. She was pleased that her husband had a change of heart about them having kids and at the rate they were going, Alyssa knew that she would be pregnant soon enough. Since Corey's apology, the newlyweds had been vibing on a different level, like they did when they first started dating. Although things were going well between them, Alyssa's suspicions of Corey wouldn't allow her to rest. He was acting as if he had nothing to hide and that nothing was bothering him, but her woman's intuition was telling her to stay woke. Instead of badgering him with questions, Alyssa played it cool because she knew if Corey was hiding something, it would come to the light eventually.

Crawling out of bed, Alyssa went into the bathroom to get ready for work. Since her first case, she had worked on a couple of cases alone before she teamed up with her co-worker on a custody case she was currently working on. An elderly couple was concerned about their grandchildren's well-being and they wanted to know if they were properly being cared for. The information that they gathered on a supposedly deadbeat mother wasn't working in their client's favor. In Alyssa's eyes, the parents were doing a hell of a job taking care of their client's grandchildren, but as she learned early on, things aren't always as good as it seems.

When she was finished in the bathroom, Alyssa wrapped a towel around her before walking into the bedroom and getting dressed. After curling her hair, she tossed everything she needed into her Louis Vuitton Never Full tote, grabbed her jacket and left her bedroom. Stopping in the kitchen to make a cup of coffee, she placed a Dunkin' Donuts k-cup in the Keurig Coffee Maker, grabbed her coffee mug from the cabinet and placed it in the cup holder. As she waited for her coffee to get finished, Alyssa heard Corey's voice coming from the guest room. Tip toeing down the hall, she leaned against the wall a few feet away from the door.

"I told you I would come see you when I could…. You'll get ya bread by the end of the week…. I done told ya ass about threatenin' me…. bye yo." He became angry.

When Corey ended his call, Alyssa quickly tipped toed back to the kitchen, removed the cup and placed the top on her cup. A few seconds later, Corey entered the kitchen wrapping his arms around her from behind. She wanted to question him about his phone call but decided against it.

"Good mornin', bae," he kissed her cheek.

"Good morning, baby. How are you doing'?" She turned around to face him.

"I'm straight," he sighed. "I don't have to be to work until the afternoon so I might be home late tonight." Corey released her.

"That's cool, bae. I'll have dinner waiting for you when you get home. Now, give me a kiss."

Alyssa gave him a quick kiss before she grabbed her things and headed out the door. Placing her things in the passenger seat, Alyssa started the car and pulled off. She arrived at her job thirty minutes later parking in the first spot she saw. Alyssa took a few moments to get her thoughts together because Corey's conversation had her confused, and as much as she wanted to inquire about it, she just left it alone. As Alyssa made her way towards the building, her partner honked the horn at her. Jogging to the car, Alyssa hopped inside the car and her partner headed to their destination for the day.

Alyssa and her co-worker spent hours following their suspects and nothing seemed to change. If the mother were mistreating the children, it would be hard to prove that with the photos and the conversations they recorded. They had a few more days to gather new evidence before they dismissed the case, but Alyssa didn't think that they would find anything that would help their client. As they headed back to the office, thoughts of Corey entered her mind as Alyssa replayed the conversation. She couldn't figure out who he could've been on the phone with that early in the morning and what type of bullshit he'd gotten himself involved in.

Who the fuck did he owe money to, she thought to herself.

The idea of her husband owing money to someone didn't sit well with her at all. Alyssa didn't want to interfere. So, she figured she'd let Corey handle the situation himself. After they arrived at the office, Alyssa and her partner stepped off the elevator and stopped to chat with the receptionist. She was telling them about the man that was in the office with Johnathan and how he was a well know lawyer in New York. They guessed why he could've been there, but before they could answer each other's questions, Johnathan's office door opened and the man shook his hand before walking out the office. Walking towards the elevator, Alyssa got a glimpse of the man's face and realized he looked familiar, but she couldn't recall where she knew him from. Alyssa stole another glance before the elevator door closed.

"Alyssa, can I see you for a moment? Johnathan asked.

"Sure," Alyssa shrugged before making her way to his office.

When she was inside, Johnathan closed the door behind her.

"What's going on?" She wore a frantic look on her face.

"Calm down, Alyssa," he chuckled. "Everything is fine. A friend of mine just left and he needs some info on a man that's dating a friend of his. I know that you're working on a case already, but I wanted to know if you would mind handling this case for me. I would handle it myself, but he wants this done asap."

"I don't mind at all." She smiled.

"Thank you. I really appreciate this."

"No problem, Johnathan."

"Here is the file and all of the details are inside. You can get started right away if you want." Johnathan handed her the file.

"I'll look over this now."

Alyssa left the office and headed over to her desk. After hanging up her jacket and her purse, she sat down at her desk and got comfortable. Opening up the file, Alyssa read over the details of the case and she damn near died when she came across D'Mari's name. Alyssa went back to the top of the page to see who was requesting this information when she saw that it was Felix Alexander. Alyssa matched the name to the face of the man that left the office. He was the lawyer that Andrea called to get Alexis out of jail after she whooped Liz's, Richard's mistress and Anastasia's ex best friend, ass. Alyssa placed her hand on her head in disbelief. It seemed like every time she started a new career, her brother-in-laws seem to pop up in her case files.

"A bitch just can't win," Alyssa mumbled to herself as she shook her head.

Question after question entered her head as she continued to read the file. Felix was requesting information on D'Mari because he's suspected to be involved with drugs and murders. After closing the folder, Alyssa placed her hands on her head rubbing her temples as she thought about why Felix was concerned about Andrea's fiancé. She had a feeling that he was up to something and that this was deeper than D'Mari being involved with a drugs and murder case. Placing the file in her purse, she jumped up from her desk, quickly leaving the office. When she reached the lobby, she pulled her phone out and called her big sister.

"Hey Hoe. What's up."

"Hey Ho-Drea. I go some shit to tell you. So, pay attention."

"Okay. I'm listening."

Chapter 11

"Diamond…. Diamond…." Lexi heard Marcus's voice in her right ear and began to wonder who he was calling.

They were standing in line waiting to get fitted for their cap and gown in the big auditorium located in the main building at Clark University. Alexis had never been more excited in her life; it had been a long four years and it was all over in a matter of months. She had been back in Atlanta for a few days now and it never failed, every time she went back home, she missed her mother and sister so much. She actually missed all her sisters which was surprising.

"Diamond… Diamond…" he whispered in her ear again, this time causing her to turn around.

"Who the fuck is Diamond and why are you calling her?" she quizzed, looking around trying to solve the mystery on her own.

"So, you trying to tell me that you don't feel like Diamond from the Player's Club? Remember the scene when she was getting fitted for her cap and gown and…."

"Shut up, Marcus," Lexi hissed, cutting him off in mid-sentence just before her name was called.

Lexi walked up to the table and provided them with her info. After flipping through a few papers that was stapled together, the older woman finally found her name. She confirmed Lexi's height as well as measured her head one final time before handing her the plastic that contained the black cap and gown. Goosebumps formed on her skin as mixed feelings and emotions plagued her mind. Lexi stood off to the side, checking her phone until Marcus was done. After they wrapped things up there, they headed to Party City.

"I can't believe Drea trusted you with these babies' gender," Marcus stated before applying a coat of his Mac lip gloss.

"The fuck is that supposed to mean?" she quizzed, eyeing him sideways.

"Honey listen, to be honest, you and yo sisters are surprising the hell outta me. Y'all went from the Kardashians to the Jackson 5," Marcus replied, smacking his lips when he was done.

"What the fuck does that supposed to mean?" Lexi chuckled, pulling into an empty parking spot.

"I have no idea chile." Marcus laughed along, unbuckling his seatbelt and exiting the vehicle.

The two best friends headed inside the large store, passing up everything, going straight to the baby section.

"Oh, my Goooddd!" Lexi cooed as she picked up anything blue and pink; plates, napkins, cups and other decorations.

"So, are the twins identical?" Marcus asked as he tossed a few things in the cart as well.

"Nope, they're fraternal, which I'm not too happy about but aye!" she said, shrugging her shoulders, while digging in her pocket to retrieve her ringing phone.

"Look, you just spoke them up," Lexi stated, showing Marcus the buzzing device as Lyssa's name flashed across the screen.

"I'm getting the pink for the gender reveal party, but she's having twin boys so I'm getting shit for the baby shower as well," she said quickly before answering her phone, not wanting her sisters to hear her conversation.

"Yoooooooo hoe!" Lexi answered, all the while still throwing items into the cart.

"I told you, Stasia. The bitch was gon answer like that. Send me my fifty dollars." Lyssa, laughed into the phone.

"Fuck y'all betting on?" Lexi quizzed.

"You and yo ratchet ass," Stasia replied, still laughing.

"Lexi, Drea told us to call you about the genders of the baby. We want to start shopping," Lyssa snickered.

"You, Drea and Stasia can go to hell. These my TT Babies; y'all bitches will find out at the gender reveal party," Lexi hissed.

"ALEXIS ARE YOU SERIOUS RIGHT NOW?" Stasia yelled.

"Dead ass serious. Now get off my phone, I'm shopping for the twins," Lexi advised them before ending the call.

After spending over three-hundred dollars on decorations, Lexi and Marcus headed to their next destination. As they drove down 285, Lexi felt her stomach growling, realizing she hadn't eaten anything the entire day, she jumped off at the next exit, making a sharp right into the parking lot of McDonalds. Although the golden arches weren't her favorite, she had a strange taste for a Big Mac, so that's what she ordered. She placed Marcus's order as well before driving forward, paying the cashier and getting her food. Lexi scrambled through the bag, popping a few fries in her mouth before heading to the club. She was meeting J.R. for the first walk-through of her new baby. The shit was still surreal to her; she couldn't believe she was going from shaking her ass to running shit, all within a year's time.

After ignoring the GPS's directions, Lexi and Marcus arrived at the club, ten minutes before they were supposed to. Lexi double checked the address when she pulled up. She had pictured the place being a little hole in the wall joint but the building she laid her eyes on was everything but that. Excitedly, Lexi jumped out the car with Marcus close behind and hurriedly approached the front door. After tugging at the black metal door, she finally pulled it open and her mouth dropped to the floor. The place was huge. The dance floor looked to hold well over five hundred people. There were two bars, one on each side of the dance floor. The stage was enormous, a long gold pole hung from the high ceiling, with a set of red curtains behind it. The DJ booth was far left of the stage and was equipped with everything needed. Lexi had only seen so little of the club, yet she was in love with it already.

"Hey baby!" J.R.'s voice sounded from behind her.

Lexi turned around, displaying the biggest smile ever.

"Oh, my God! Baby, I love it!" She cooed, running into his arms.

J.R. picked her up off the ground, wrapping his big arms around her before placing her back on her feet.

"All I gotta do is add a little Sexi Lexi to it and BOOM…. We in this bitch!" she exclaimed.

"I'm glad you like it." J.R. smiled, rubbing his hands through the small goatee he began to grow.

"I think you should have some male strippers too, best friend," Marcus finally spoke.

"Nah big fella, we good on the niggas," J.R. replied, causing Marcus to frown up his face.

"This day has been awesome. First, I get my cap and gown and then I shop for my nephews and now this," she beamed, turning around in a full circle with her hands raised in the air.

"Shit only gon get better, baby. Let me show you the rest," J.R. replied, smacking Lexi on the ass before they dipped off to where the back offices were located.

Lexi's office was the size of her bedroom back home. A huge cherry Oakwood desk sat pretty in the middle of the marble floor. A maroon leather couch along with a chaise completed the décor. Lexi designed the room in her head. The more and more ideas she came up with, the more excited she got.

"So, you came up with a name yet?" J.R. quizzed as he grabbed her by the waist, pulling her between his legs as he sat leaned against the desk.

"Nope, not yet, but I been thinking." She smiled, sneaking a kiss.

"Whatever you come up with. It's gon be epic."

"Thanks baby and if I never told you before, I love you and I appreciate all you do for me," Lexi yelped before grabbing her stomach as a sharp pain shot through it.

"You ok?" a concerned J.R. asked.

"Yeah, my stomach just started hurting all of a sud….."

Lexi's words were cut short by the vomit that suddenly formed in her mouth. She took off running down the hall, pushing open every door until she found the bathroom. Only being able to make it to the sink, Lexi dumped out the McDonalds she consumed only minutes ago.

"You ok?" J.R. appeared behind her and questioned.

"Yeah I'm…"

Lexi gagged again but this time, nothing came up.

"Damn shorty, you straight?"

"Yeah, I hope so," Lexi replied, turning on the water in the facet, splashing it on her face.

After popping a stick of gum in her mouth, she headed back to where she had left Marcus. He was sitting on top of the bar, his face buried in his phone as his legs swung back and forth.

"Boy if you don't get yo ass down," Lexi scolded as Marcus hopped down with a quickness.

The three of them wrapped up things there before heading out. Lexi did one final walk through and that's when it hit her.

"HS4," she blurted out, causing J.R. and Marcus to stare at her.

"What the fuck is you talking about?" Marcus quizzed.

"The name of my club is HS4!" she repeated proudly, thinking about the meaning behind the name.

Chapter 12

"If you tell me, I promise I'll act surprised at the Gender Reveal," Drea pleaded with Lexi.

"Nooooo, Andrea Holiday and stop asking meee!!" Lexi expressed.

"You make me so sick," Drea rolled her eyes and flipped Lexi off and then ended the FaceTime call while Lexi was laughing in her face.

The phone rang again instantly and Drea knew why.

"I'm sorry, Lexi," she said right away.

"Yeah you better be. For a bitch that don't like to get hung up on, how you gon do the shit to somebody else?"

"I said I'm sorry... now bye. I think I'm bout to fly to New York to surprise my man," Drea smiled.

"Drea, that's a long ass way to fly and surprise somebody. You acting like me now... but you know what... yeah, go get you some dick because you need it."

"Bye, Alexis Holiday."

Drea hung up the phone and couldn't help but laugh at her baby sister. That girl was gonna be crazy for the rest of her life and everyone might as well accept it. She had been thinking about it since the day before, and instantly decided that it was time to see her fiancé. The long-distance thing was getting harder and harder. Drea knew that D'Mari would probably be a little upset about her flying, but he would get over it once she sucked his dick real good and put her pussy on him. Her pregnancy hormones had her hornier than ever and Drea found herself feenin' for her man all the damn time. Phone sex was cool and all, but it was no comparison to the real thing.

There was actually a flight leaving Jackson at two o'clock the next morning that was nonstop to LaGuardia. Drea was surprised as hell that there was no connecting flight. Even though the flight cost almost eight hundred dollars, she booked it and went and started packing. It was a four-hour flight, but that was cool because with the time change, Drea knew that she would be able to catch D'Mari before he even left home. Her pussy got wet at just the thought. After Drea was packed, she got the sudden urge for some Burger King. Her mom always made sure she was eating good, but a whopper with cheese was on her mind, so she decided to go and get something to eat since there was a Burger King right down the street. As soon as Drea got in the car, her phone rang and she saw that it was D'Mari and smiled.

"Hey baby," she cooed.

"Hey love… how y'all doing?"

"We're good. I just got in the car and headed to Burger King. Then I'm coming back home to catch up on my show, *The Have and The Have Nots*. What you doing?"

"Shit… the usual. Missing you."

"Aww baby, I miss you, too. This distance is killing me. I need you here with me," Drea admitted.

"I know… I'm gonna get back to you soon. Just gotta make sure some shit is straight. I got a few things to handle. You know how it goes."

"Yeah, I understand… hold on let me order my food right quick," Drea told him after she pulled up and was asked to place her order.

"Yes, may I have a number one with cheese, no onions… with a coke and also a Hershey pie… that's all."

"You just made me want some damn Burger King girl," D'Mari laughed.

They chatted until Drea paid for her food at one window, but D'Mani beeped in when she made it to the next window and D'Mari told her that he would call her back. She retrieved her food and pulled off. Something told Drea to check her bag, and when she did she noticed that her Hershey pie wasn't inside. She pulled up and parked and then went inside. Before she could make it to the counter, one of the workers started heading her way with a bag. The girl apologized and Drea told her it was fine, even though she was a little agitated. She knew that mistakes happened, she was just glad that she noticed it before she made it back home. When Drea made it to the door, she was met by an older man. She could tell that he had to have been quite the player back in his younger days.

"Whooo you look like you need me to bend you over and put another baby in you!" he said and Drea was shocked as hell by his comment, but she couldn't even get mad. She laughed at him.

"Get back, old man." She pushed by him.

"When ya baby daddy start acting up... come and find Ronald," he called out to her.

A thought popped into Drea's head, so she turned around.

"Pull your phone out old pimp and call this number. I got the perfect match just for you."

Drea gave him the number and walked back to her car while laughing.

"What's my future wife name so I can save it?"

"Shirley," Drea called out to him and disappeared.

Drea didn't know how far Ronald would get with Aunt Shirley, but she couldn't wait to hear about it.

***

A little after seven o'clock the next morning, Drea was headed to baggage claim. She tried not to over pack since she was only planning on staying a few days, but she still ended up with more stuff than could fit in one of her carry-on luggages. Drea went to the Uber app on her phone and requested one as soon as she got her suitcase. She knew that there would be plenty at the airport already, which was why she waited until she was about to head out. Her phone rang a few moments later and Drea was informed to look for a black Maxima. As soon as she walked out, she spotted it and a man hopped out and grabbed her luggage and threw it in the trunk. Drea got comfortable and smiled at thoughts of seeing her baby. She sent a message to the Holiday Sisters group chat letting them know that she had arrived in New York and then closed her eyes in an attempt to contain her excitement about seeing D'Mari's face after he laid eyes on her.

Drea didn't know that she had dosed off to sleep until the driver stopped and woke her up. She looked up and saw that she was at her destination and then smiled.

"Can you wait a couple of minutes before you pull off. I think someone is here, but I just need to make sure," Drea told the Uber driver before he could get out and get her luggage out of the trunk.

Once he agreed, she got out and headed for the door. She knew what type of life D'Mari lived, so the possibility of him being gone was strong as hell. He often told her that he lived his life by one of Jeezy's saying, "sleep when you die." There was no way in hell she would do that because she needed her sleep and was definitely going to get it. Drea pranced to the front door dressed in an Adidas jogger and shoes to match. She was dressed comfortable for her flight and not sexy, but D'Mari's ass better be happy to see her no matter what. Drea rang the doorbell and stood there feeling like a school girl with butterflies in her stomach. Just when she was about to ring the doorbell again, the door opened and there stood one of the most beautiful women she had ever seen in her life.

A lump formed in Drea's throat as several thoughts ran through her mind. *Why is this bitch answering D'Mari's door this early in the morning? Why the hell does she only have on a wife beater? Is it his shirt?* All of those questions plus more ran through Drea's mind before the girl spoke and interrupted her.

"Who are you and why are you here so early like you belong here?"

"Who are you?" Drea snapped back because she didn't like the tone that the bitch was using.

"Not that it's any of your concern, but I'm Dina… now who the fuck are you and why are you at D'Mari's door so early in the morning?" Dina stepped towards her.

Drea wanted to snap, but considering the shape that she was in, she decided to take the high road and just leave. Clearly the bitch belonged there if she came at her sideways and shit.

"Dina, who you talking to?" she heard D'Mari call out, but Drea was headed back to the Uber with tears streaming down her face.

"Some lost looking bitch…" Dina said.

"Drea… wait Drea," D'Mari called after her, but Drea hurriedly got in the car and left.

"Pull off please," she told the driver while she was in tears.

He did as she requested and Drea looked up and saw D'Mari trying to stop her. The only thing he had on was a pair of Nike basketball shorts and Drea couldn't help but to wonder what she had interrupted. She gave the Uber driver Stasia'a address and cried the whole way there. When the driver pulled up, she didn't stop him when he got out to get her luggage. She banged on Anastasia's door and after a minute or so, it flung open and she locked eyes with D'Mani.

"What's wrong, sis?" he asked.

"Ask your cheating ass brother," Drea snapped and walked by him and into the house.

"What's wrong, Drea? You been crying?" Stasia appeared.

"My brother and I might be a lot of thangs, but cheating ain't one of them… I hope we can say the same about y'all, too," D'Mani said and Drea caught the shade and wondered what else had transpired between her sister and D'Mani. Drea caught the look that Stasia gave him and knew that something had definitely happened.

"What happened, Drea?" Stasia quizzed.

Drea ran the story down to her sister and when she said Dina's name, D'Mani cut her off.

"Dina in town? Drea, Dina is our lil feisty ass cousin from Jamaica. He probably didn't get a chance to tell her about you and she was being the overprotective cousin that she's always been.

After D'Mani said that, Drea thought about the chick and she did have an accent.

"Oh, my God…I overreacted and just left for no reason," Drea sighed.

"Well, if a bitch answered my man door I would act the same way, sis. Calm down, it'll be alright. Plus, you have a reason to be emotional," Stasia comforted her.

Drea continued to cry in her sister's arm. She felt stupid for not waiting to at least hear D'Mari out. Stasia rubbed Drea's back and a few minutes later she felt strong hands pulling her back.

"Stop that crying and come here girl," D'Mari pulled her close.

"I'm sorry I didn't wait… I just wanted to surprise you," she sobbed.

"Calm down, girl… we'll talk about all that later. And the fact that you hopped on a plane without telling me," he lifted her chin.

"I was missing you," she admitted.

D'mari kissed her and Drea knew that she had made the right decision by making a trip to see him.

"You two get a room," Stasis interrupted them and Drea laughed.

"Come on, let's go back to my house," D'Mari said and that was all Drea needed to hear to make her clit throb.

Chapter 13

Anastasia eased out of bed when she finally heard Kyler's low snores. She was glad that it had only taken one bedtime story for him to go to sleep and she had to deliver it since she had made him a promise. Since he was asleep, her and D'Mani could have some alone time. Ever since the night Zyree had sent that dress and shit D'Mani had been giving her the cold shoulder. He wouldn't even let her anywhere near the dick. She didn't know how much longer he could hold out and she wasn't trying to find out either. Going from having sex multiple times a day to not getting any at all had Anastasia moody as fuck. She was snappy, irritable and every other word in between, and he was just going around living life. She hoped that tonight that shit would be over though because they were leaving the next morning heading to Atlanta for Lexi's graduation and Stasia wanted to be on good terms with her man.

Anastasia could hear the shower running when she entered their bedroom. She couldn't help but think that God had to be on her side as she stripped down to nothing and entered the steamy bathroom. She slowly made her way to the shower and slid the door back with a sexy smile plastered over her face. At the sound of the door opening D'Mani looked her way. His eyes grazed her body from head to toe, as she did the same. The way the soapy water rolled down his skin had Anastasia licking her lips in anticipation, but as fast as she had his attention she lost it. Without saying a word D'Mani turned away and continued to run the washcloth over his body. That shit didn't do anything but make Anastasia want to touch him more. She took his silence as an invitation and stepped inside of the roomy shower behind him. Pressing her body against his, she planted a kiss between his shoulder blades and wrapped her arms around his waist.

"Are you still mad at me?" she asked almost afraid of his response. As much as she had been through to have D'Mani, the last thing she wanted was for Zyree to come between them.

"Nah, you straight." he said flatly shrugging out of her arms.

"What the fuck is that supposed to mean, D'Mani?" she fumed with her hands on her hips. How was she "straight" if his ass still wouldn't let her touch him?

"It mean just what I said, you straight," he tossed over

his shoulder and then shut the water off, before stepping out.

Anastasia stood there shocked, watching with her mouth dropped open, as he wrapped a towel around himself, and walked out of the bathroom. It was obvious he was still feeling some type of way about the situation. She could understand him being upset, but it had been too long, and she was not about to play with him. Granted she should have just told him about Zyree's advances, but in her defense, she didn't want him to harm Kyler's daddy over something so small, and besides that it wasn't like she was encouraging him.

Anastasia hurried to cut the water back on and washed her body a few times before she followed him out of the shower. She was determined to get back on his good side no matter what. When she returned to the room she found D'Mani in bed lying on his back with one arm stretched behind his head and the other resting on his stomach. The sight of him lying there comfortably irritated her. For one, she knew his ass wasn't sleep and for two she knew he missed her just as much as she missed him and was just being difficult. Crossing the room, she climbed on top of him, making his eyes pop open. She could feel his semi-erect dick poking her through the cover and she smirked down at him knowingly, unfazed by the scowl on his face.

"Get yo ass off me, Stasia!" he fussed and wiped pretend sleep from his eyes.

"No! Not until you give me what I want!" she said causing a laugh to erupt from deep in his belly.

"Fuck you think you bouta just take the dick?" he questioned with humor in his tone.

"If I have to." She shrugged and dropped her towel, then grinded against him.

"Man, watch out." He smirked, barely bucking beneath her.

"No," Anastasia whined. She leaned down and started licking and sucking on his neck. "You said you're not mad anymore, prove it." She knew that was his spot. After she felt him give up the little bit of fight he had left, she spun around into the sixty-nine position, and put as much of his growing dick into her mouth as she could.

It didn't take long for him to get into it and return the favor. As usual the pleasure that D'Mani delivered with his tongue made it difficult for her to finish.

"Oooh shit, D'Mani!" she panted, grinding into his face. Anastasia could already feel her orgasm threatening to erupt, as D'Mani held her in place and assaulted her clit. All that could be heard throughout the room was the sound of Anastasia's light moaning and D'Mani lapping at her wetness.

Anastasia's eyes rolled into the back of her head as she exploded all over his face. She couldn't even move as her body twitched involuntarily, but D'Mani wasn't done with her yet. With little effort he had her on her knees, and he slid inside of her with ease.

"Shiiiiit Mani!"

"Shut yo ass up! You said you wanted the dick, you gone get it. Now, toot that ass for daddy," D'Mani grunted, slapping her on the ass as he continued to deliver back strokes that had Stasia grabbing at the bedspread. He grabbed a handful of her hair and pulled her head back so that he could kiss her roughly. Anastasia bit into her lip to keep herself from crying out and waking up Kyler, because D'Mani was making up for lost time.

"You missed this shit, huh?"

"Yessssss!"

"I bet you did, next time I ask you some shit you better tell me the truth!" he demanded, slamming into her with each word.

"Okaay!" Anastasia screeched as her stomach tightened with another orgasm.

"Okay what?"

"Okay daddy!"

"Fuuuuuck." D'Mani couldn't help but moan as he watched his dick begin to glisten from her wetness. It wasn't long before he had emptied his seeds deep inside of her and laid back to catch his breath. Anastasia moved up in the bed and cuddled next to him laying her head on his chest.

"I wasn't playin, Stasia. Don't keep shit else from me, yo baby daddy violatin and as a man I need to handle that shit. So, let me do that."

"I'm sorry, I promise I won't keep nothing else from you when it comes to Zyree," Anastasia promised, ready to put the whole ordeal behind them.

Chapter 14

"Our Uber will be here in ten minutes to take us to the airport," Corey announced from the living room. "Did you pack everythin' you need, Lyssa?"

"I'm double checking now, bae," she yelled back to him making sure she had everything.

After tossing a few things in her suitcase, Alyssa zipped it closed before placing on her shades and leaving out the room. Flopping down on the sofa, she pulled her phone out of her pocket to check in with her sisters.

Lyssa: My Uber should be here in a few. We'll meet y'all at the airport, Stasia.

Stasia: Cool.

Drea: I'll meet y'all at the hotel. D'Mari is already on his way here and mama and aunt Shirley should be arriving the same time as y'all.

Lexi: Y'all hoes better be well rested cuz we turning the fuck up this weekend.

Lyssa: Ayyeee!!

Stasia: I can't wait!

Drea: Y'all asses know I can't do too much but I'm gon do what I can.

Alyssa laughed at her sister's comments before tucking her phone in the pocket of her Bermuda shorts. She hadn't seen her sisters since their vacation and Alyssa was beyond excited to see them this weekend. It was Lexi's graduation weekend and they were hype about their baby sister getting her degree. Besides Baby Holiday's graduation celebration, it was also Andrea's gender reveal party. Alyssa couldn't wait to find out if she was having twin nieces or nephews.

Minutes later, their Uber arrived and Alyssa locked up the house while Corey placed their suitcases in the trunk. Alyssa hopped in the backseat and Corey slid in next to her closing the door shut. As they rode to the airport, the couple held hands while they looked out the window. Since she eavesdropped on Corey's conversation, he seemed less stressed and in a better mood. The feeling that had been haunting her was slowly fading but until it was fully gone, Alyssa was going to stay cautious. Besides her problems with Corey, she was concerned about Drea and the information she shared with her about the case. Alyssa knew her sister was a little shaken by the news but like always, Drea played it cool. With her marital and work problems, Alyssa was ready to forget about all that shit this weekend and just enjoy herself.

They arrived at the John F. Kennedy International Airport thirty minutes later and after thanking their driver, Corey grabbed the bags out the car before making their way inside to check their bags. When they arrived at their gate, the couple spotted Anastasia, D'Mani and Kyler sitting in the waiting area. Stasia was first to see them and jumped to her feet giving her sister a big hug before doing the same to her brother-in-law. They chatted until it was time for them to board the plane a few minutes later. Once they were comfortably seated, Alyssa placed her earphones in her ear putting on her tunes. Linking her arm with Corey's, she placed her head on his shoulder and quickly drifted off to sleep.

Two and half hours later, Corey was waking her up to get off the plane. When they stepped off the plane, Kyler grabbed her hand as they headed to baggage claim to pick up their luggage. Grabbing their luggage off the conveyer belt, they headed over to Enterprise to pick up their rentals for the weekend. After the receptionist handed the men their keys, the couples went to their trucks, loaded them with their bags, hopped in and drove to the hotel. They were all staying at the Embassy Suites that was located at Centennial Olympic Park. As Alyssa navigated Corey to the hotel, she sent a text message to her sisters letting them know that they would be arriving at the hotel soon. Andrea texted them her room number for Alyssa and Anastasia to join her and Lexi in her room when they got there.

When Corey parked the car, she gave her man a quick kiss on the lips and told him to text her their room number before linking arms with her sister and catching the elevator to the fifth floor to Drea's room. Stepping off the elevator, they found her room and knocked on the door. Seconds later, D'Mari opened the door and they greeted their soon to be brother- in-law with a hug. As they entered the room, they saw J.R. sitting on the couch and hugged him before walking to the bedroom where their sisters were.

"Hey Hoes!" Lexi shouted when they walked through the door.

They all shouted different greetings as they embraced each other in a group hug. It felt good to be in the company of her sisters and it seemed like whatever problems she came there with instantly vanished.

"I missed y'all hoes." Andrea sat back down on the bed putting her feet up.

"Same here," Lyssa smiled.

"Me too," Stasia agreed.

"I low key missed y'all asses too but not that much though," Lexi stated before sitting next to her Drea.

"Fuck you, Lexi," Lyssa and Stasia said in unison causing them to laugh.

"So, what was y'all talking about? I know y'all planning something for the night?" Anastasia sat on the end of the bed along with Alyssa.

"We can just chill here and turn up," Lexi shrugged.

"That's cool with me," Stasis agreed.

"That works," Alyssa chimed in.

"Well, we know what we're doing later but it's only 2:15pm though. What are we gonna do until then?" Drea questioned.

They sat in silence for a moment as they thought of something to do.

"Pool," they said in unison.

They agreed to meet each other at the pool before Alyssa and Anastasia got up to leave.

"Oh. Just to let y'all know, y'all have to be at the stadium tomorrow no later than 7:30am. So, try to get there early so everyone can sit together," Lexi informed them.

"Damn! What time does it start?" Alyssa shouted.

"At 8 a.m. I gotta be there the same time as y'all. So, what the fuck you complaining for?" Lexi placed a hand on her hip.

"It makes sense for you to be there early. It's your graduation, but if a bitch gotta wake up before Jesus and the Mexicans to see her baby sister graduate, then so be it," Alyssa smiled.

The Holiday sisters burst into laughter at Alyssa's statement before her and Anastasia left to change into their swimsuits. Checking her phone, she had a text from Corey letting her know that they were in room 510 which was a couple doors away from Andrea's room and Anastasia was in room 504. Alyssa walked into the room and smiled when she saw that Corey had her swimsuit, Chanel slides and cover-up waiting for her on the bed. After changing into her swim wear, Alyssa placed her Chanel shades on her face before grabbing her phone and heading out the room. When she made it the pool area, she saw that Corey was already there. She watched as he did laps in the pool. Kicking her slides off and removing her cover-up, Alyssa got in the pool and instantly got his attention. They began kissing like they were the only ones in the pool until her sisters showed up seconds later interrupting their moment.

The sisters, their men and Kyler were having a good time in the pool as they splashed and dunked each other. Andrea and D'Mari were hugged up in the pool in their own little world. Alyssa was about to tell them to get a room before Aunt Shirley walked in beating her to the punch with Victoria in tow.

Everyone shouted different greetings as the two women got comfortable in the lounge chairs. Spending a couple of more hours in the pool, they all decided to get out and rest up before they went out to dinner. Making it to their room, Alyssa headed straight to the bathroom and Corey was on her heels. Alyssa knew what he wanted and she quickly gave into his advances.

After fucking for a few rounds, the couple washed up and got dressed for the get together they were having in Drea's room. J.R. and D'Mari went to go get drinks while Corey and D'Mani went to go get food. Alexis and Aunt Shirley left to go smoke while Andrea, Anastasia and Alyssa stayed in the room dancing to music. Stasia and Lyssa laughed as Drea tried to drop it low with her big belly. Minutes later, the men, Aunt Shirley and Lexi came into the room with a bucket of ice, food, alcohol, paper plates and cups. Aunt Shirley downed the alcohol that was in her flask before snatching the bottle of Henny from the bag and refilled it. When *Nice for What* by Drake came on, Lexi moved everybody out her way so she could do what she did best, which was twerk. It wasn't long before Aunt Shirley joined her favorite niece and dropped it like it was hot. Alyssa's mouth hit the floor when Aunt Shirley started twerking on D'Mari and even though he tried to swerve her, she followed him all around the room until Andrea stepped in and shut shit down. The ladies danced with their spouses for a few songs before they decided to eat and play drinking games. A few hours later, everyone decided to call it a night because they had to be up early for Lexi's big day.

Besides the blaring alarm clock waking her up at four in the morning, Andrea went to everyone's room making sure everyone was up. Alyssa's head was throbbing from the hangover she had. She wanted to pull the covers over her head and go back to sleep but Alyssa rolled her ass out of bed and got ready for the long day ahead of them. After Corey zipped up her white off the shoulder dress that stopped at her knee, Alyssa slipped her feet in silver spiked Christian Louboutin's shoes. She put on her diamond hoops and tennis bracelet, tossed her things in her clutch and left out the room with Corey on her heels, D'Mani, Stasia, Aunt Shirley and Victoria were waiting in the hallway. Everyone was wearing white and they all looked fly as fuck.

"If Drea don't hurry her ass up, I'm goin' back in my room and goin' to sleep," Aunt Shirley fussed. "I thought Lexi was bullshittin' when she said we had to be up at the crack of dawn."

"Shirley, stop ya damn complain'. My baby girl is graduatin' today so keep your fuckery to a minimum."

The sisters giggled while Aunt Shirley flipped their mom the bird behind her back. A few minutes later, Andrea and D'Mari joined them in the hallway and they rode the elevator to the lobby before strolling out the door to parking lot. Victoria hopped in the car with Andrea while Aunt Shirley rode Alyssa, Anastasia and Corey in D'Mani's truck. They rode quietly in the car as the GPS guided them to their destination. They arrived at the Panthers Stadium a half hour later and there were already cars in the parking lot. Finding a spot close to the entrance, D'Mani parked and his twin parked in the spot next to him. They climbed out the car and spotted J.R. as they made their way towards that entrance. The ushers handed them programs on their way in and everyone moaned and complained about walking up the steps to the stands but they got good enough seats where they could see everything clear. They had the seats set up on the field for the graduates and the red carpet in the middle of the aisle for them to walk on.

At 8:00 on the nose, the graduation began. They showed the graduates making their way to the stadium on the screens they had up on each side of the field as the choir sang. Minutes later, the graduates entered the stadium and everyone began to clap. When they spotted Lexi, they shouted her name causing her to look in their direction and waved at them. When the choir was finished singing their selection, the graduates sat down in their seats. As the ceremony went on, it was hard for Alyssa to keep her eyes open. Every time she dozed off, either Andrea or Corey were waking her up. They even had to wake Aunt Shirley's ass up a few times as well. When they announced that they were about to hand out the degrees, everyone was wide awake. The sisters waited anxiously for the announcer to call Lexi's name. They watched as their sister walked up the steps and onto the stage. When her name was called, the sisters jumped to their feet and hit the Nae-Nae right along with Lexi as the family cheered her on.

When the graduation was over, they stayed close together as they made their way out the stadium. J.R. told the family to wait for him while he went to find Lexi.

"I can't believe y'all carried on like that when they called my baby's name," Victoria chuckled. "That girl couldn't be normal for one day."

"Now you know how Lexi is, mama and you know we weren't gonna let her act a fool alone," Alyssa kissed her mother's cheek.

"Well fuck all y'all for not includin' me in the dance. Y'all always leavin' me out of shit. Raggedy ass heffas."

The sisters laughed at Aunt Shirley's comment which didn't bother neither one of them at all. Moments later, Lexi and J.R. made their way through the crowd of people and she gave Victoria a big hug before sharing a group hug with her sisters. After everyone showered her with hugs and praises, the family made their way to their cars and Alexis told them that she would text them the address to where the gender reveal party was being held. Once they were in their cars, D'Mani followed the rest of the cars out of the lot. Alyssa, just like the rest of the family, was happy for her sister. She was glad that they all decided to put their problems behind them because if they were still at odds, Alyssa would've missed one of the happiest moments of her baby sister's life. Now that the graduation was over, it was time for them to celebrate some more as they waited to find out the gender of Andrea and D'Mari's twins.

Chapter 15

"It's ovvverrrr nowwwwww. It's oveeeeerrrr nowwwwww. I feel like I can make it. The storm is over now!" Lexi sang acapella at the top of her lungs as her and the family headed to J.R.'s house about twenty minutes from where her graduation was held.

"LEXI SHUT UP!" Everyone yelled out at her but she didn't pay them any mind.

She was the happiest she had ever been, she was on a natural high, although it wasn't better than weed; it was close.

"Lexi, are you sure everything is set up?" Drea asked from the back seat as they did sixty-five down 285.

"Yes Dreaaaaaa." Lexi rolled her eyes.

"My home girl is there to let everyone in. I set up mostly everything last night so chill. Damn!" Lexi cursed.

Drea flipped her the bird, causing everyone to laugh. Lexi turned around in her seat and looked out the back window. Although J.R. was flying, Corey was keeping up in the other car. She couldn't wait to get to their destination where the turn-up would begin. She had worked so hard on the gender reveal party, she couldn't wait for everyone to see.

Arriving about thirty minutes later, Lexi hopped out of the truck with her spiked Christian Louboutin's in hand and headed to J.R.'s two story brick home. It had been a minute since either of them had spent time there, since he was always at her place but it was much bigger and the party was being held in the backyard.

"WAIIITTTTT!!" Lexi yelled to everyone who made their way to the house before her.

Everyone stopped and stayed put until she jogged across the lawn bare foot. She went inside her purse, grabbed her key before slipping inside the front door. Once inside she went and grabbed a glass bowl off of the living room table and bought it back outside with her.

"Ok, listen up! I have these pins. A blue one, a pink one, as well as a double sided one with blue and pink. If you are team twin boys, grab blue, if you are team twin girls, grab a pink and if you…. Y'all know the rest, just grab a pin. The side gate is open, everyone can go through there," Lexi instructed while her immediate family as well as other family members, along with Drea's co-workers and friends filled in.

The backyard was set up beautifully. Lexi hired the best party planner in Atlanta and looking at the final results, it was well worth the couple of thousands she spent. She glanced over at Drea who had wobbled in and smiled. Her big sister was in tears looking at the gorgeous set up. The backyard was decorated in gold, everything from the lights that hung from the gate to the gold ribbons that wrapped around the white lawn chairs. The centerpiece at each table was a picture of the babies' ultrasound, with a blue and pink ribbon covering the private parts. The waitress and waiter, made their way around, taking drink orders while they waited for more guest to arrive.

"Baby Holiday, I must say, you did yo thang," Stasia said, admiring the details of the backyard.

"Well thank you!" Lexi replied, smiling from ear to ear.

"This shit is beautiful, but do we really have to find out when everyone else does?" Lyssa quizzed.

"Girl yes…. The fuck…. Everybody will know in about an hour so be cool." Lexi informed her.

Both sisters smacked their lips as Drea walked over and joined the circle.

"I absolutely love this," Drea beamed, as she pulled her younger sister into a hug.

"Well, with no help from these other bitches, I did do my thang didn't I," she boasted, winking her eye at both Stasia and Lyssa.

Lexi threw the whole shade tree at her two other sisters who frowned their faces and called her a few bitches under their breath.

"What y'all over here talking about?" Corey walked over and questioned, pulling Lyssa into a bear hug from the back.

"Aye Lexi, thanks. I ain't never seen no shit set up like this," Mari added in, followed by D'Mani and J.R. who both walked up with cups of liquor in their hands.

"Thanks y'all. I've been so excited and I can't wait to meet the bo…. The twins." Lexi said, stopping herself before giving the babies genders away.

Everybody noticed the fuck up because they all eyed her suspiciously but the look on Lexi's face, dared them to say something. Just as she was about to go off, Aunt Shirley joined their circle with her best friend in hand, her flask.

"What y'all hoes got going on?" she stuttered.

"Who you calling a hoe?" Drea asked, placing her hands on her hips.

"Well, you pregnant from a one-night stand. Anastasia…. Please don't get me started on you…. Alyssa, you got yo shit together the most but you still got some hoe-tendencies and Lexi…"

"Lexi what?" she interrupted.

"You just living your best life," Shirley laughed, causing everyone else to follow suit.

"So, Auntie, what's been going on?" D'Mari asked, placing his arm around her shoulders.

"Nah nigga, don't touch me now." Shirley curved him, removing his arm.

"When I wanted you… yo brother…. Yo cousin AND J.R., none of y'all niggaz wanted me but ooohhhh since I got a man now, y'all all up on me!" Shirley snapped.

"Wait! What?" Lyssa laughed.

"You ain't the only one who can get a nigga to marry them," Shirley hissed.

"Auntie, you got a man?" Stasia questioned.

"I sure do and here he come right now!"

The Holiday sisters along with their men, looked around the backyard, trying to find this mystery man. Luckily for them, they didn't have to look far before an older man, with a gray goatee, wearing a pair of tan corduroys, a black blazer with a t-shirt underneath and some gray cowboy boots walked towards them. Aunt Shirley fixed her hair and pulled up the pink and yellow sunflower dress she was wearing.

"Hey Daddy," Shirley gushed as everyone tried to hold in their breakfast.

"Auntie this you?" Lexi grinned as she stuck out her tongue and did a little dance.

"Fine ain't he niece?" Shirley replied before introducing everybody.

Turns out, that Andrea gave him Shirley's phone number and they actually hit it off. The man flew all the way from

Mississippi just to be with her. The shit was nasty but cute in its own little way.

"So, Auntie, cuz you got a new man now, you ain't fuckn with me either?" J.R. asked, still shooting his shot.

"Jeremy… My Jeremy. Back then you didn't want me. Now I'm hot, you all up on me," Shirley replied, reciting an old Mike Jones song before taking a sip from her flask.

"Girl, shut up. You so rude. Hello, I'm Anastasia," Stasia said, extending her hand for a handshake.

"Hello, I'm Ronald. You the one who don't know who yo baby daddy is, right?" Ronald took Stasia's hand and shook it.

"Really Auntie?" she shouted.

"What? Don't you tell yo man secrets?" Shirley asked.

"Well, I'm Lexi and whatever this old heffa told you about me, is probably true." Lexi smiled, shaking his hand as well.

"Oh, so you the gay stripper? Sorry to hear about the recent loss of your girlfriend," he apologized sincerely.

"Shirley, you out here telling my sister's business. What's wrong with you?" Lyssa questioned.

"You the snitch, not me," Shirley corrected her.

"Oh, so this must be the crooked agent. Which means the pregnant one is the lawyer whor..."

"Hold up old head, watch yo mouth." D'Mari stepped in before Ronald could go any further.

"I don't want no trouble young man. I just feel like I know them already," Ronald said, holding both hands in the air, as if he was surrendering.

"Look, let's get this shit started. I say we do the reveal and then eat. Let's go!" Lexi told the crew before heading over to where the DJ was.

Lexi grabbed the mic as he cut the music off. She cleared her throat before speaking.

"I just want to thank everyone for coming out today. Can I have Drea and Mari come forward?"

The guest all cheered and smiled as D'Mari held Drea's hand as they made their way to the front.

"Ok, so being that this is the first set of twins in our family, I wanted to do something different. I need everyone to direct their attention to the sky."

As soon as Lexi gave those instructions. Two small jet planes started circling the air. Both planes releasing different color smokes. Lexi looked over at her sister who was gushing with excitement. Just as both planes released blue smoke, the guest erupted and so did D'Mari, but Drea had a strange look on her face. Just as Lexi was about to say something, Drea fainted and hit the ground.

Chapter 16

Everyone was laughing and having a good time, but out of nowhere, pain took over Drea's body and all she could do was scream and fall to the ground with tears streaming down her face. She heard people calling her name and pulling at her, but after Drea made impact with the ground, darkness consumed her entire world.

"The terbutaline didn't work... we have to prep for delivery now!"

Drea heard those words as soon as she woke up and panicked.

"Oh, my God... what's wrong? What's going on? Are my babies okay? Where's D'Mari and my sisters?" Drea asked question after question after question.

"Calm down, sweetie!" A nurse rubbed her shoulders.

"Her blood pressure is elevating and the heart rates are dropping. We have to hurry!"

Tears poured down Drea's cheeks nonstop. She had been having the time of her life with her family and it led to something that seems devastating. A few pains had hit her, but she thought they were just Braxton hick's contractions that she had read about. Apparently, they were real contractions because they were prepping her for surgery. The more the doctors and the nurses hurried around, the more Drea panicked.

"We're losing the babies!" some screamed.

"NOOOOOO," Drea let out a gutwrenching scream and the next thing she knew, she was being given a shot and it was lights out.

***

Drea didn't know how much time had passed, but when she woke up, tears were still streaming down her face. Someone wiped her tears away and she looked up and locked eyes with D'Mari. He leaned down and hugged her and it made Drea cry harder. In her heart, she felt like something was wrong, but she was afraid to ask any questions. Since D'Mari didn't say anything, she finally found her voice even though it cracked after every word.

"Whe... where... are... m... my... babies?"

"They put us out baby, but they want you to remain calm," D' Mari tried to comfort her.

"No…I gotta find my babies," Drea protested and tried to stand up.

D'Mari gently but firmly held her in place.

"Drea, you just gave birth so you gotta be careful. Ima go and get some answers, but I wanted to be here when you woke up. Your sisters and mom and them are out there. I'm sure someone will come in and give us an update soon," D'Mari said.

Before anything else could be said, the room door swung open and in walked the Holiday Sisters with Lexi leading the pack. They all rushed towards the bed and wrapped their arms around Drea, pretty much pushing D'Mari out of the way.

"Aww sisterrrr… they wouldn't let us in, but you really had the babies," Lexi noted.

"They are sooo tiny," Lyssa added.

"We couldn't tell the sex of them because they pushed us out," Stasia chimed in.

"Are they okay?" Drea sniffled.

"They are fine. We have to keep the faith," Victoria made her presence known.

No one even saw her or Aunt Shirley walk in.

"Mama, please go see if they are okay. What did I do wrong?" Drea's tears came back once her mom made it over to her.

"Those babies are gonna be just fine," Victoria comforted her oldest daughter.

"Yeah, Drea, my little nephews are gon' be just fine. Stay strong," Lexi said.

"We got two boys?" D'Mari excitedly quizzed.

"Lexi, we been asking you all day what the genders were," Stasia fussed.

"Y'all know I wasn't gon tell y'all hoes… I mean y'all know I wasn't gon tell y'all before I told Drea." Lexi rolled her eyes and a little laughter finally fell upon the room.

Before anyone could say anything else, a doctor walked into the room and everyone got quiet. You could literally hear a pin drop; the room was just that quiet.

"Ms. Holiday… you gave us quite a scare, but I'm happy to announce that your baby boy and baby girl are going to be okay. They are in the NICU, and they will be there for a little while, but we see no reason that they won't pull through. That little boy is very strong, the chord was wrapped around his neck and we had to bring him back, but he's just fine now."

There wasn't a dry eye in the room by the time the doctor was done talking. Drea was finally able to release the breath that she was holding once the doctor told her that Baby A, which was the girl weighed in at two pounds and six ounces and Baby B, the boy weighed in at three pounds and ten ounces.

"A boy and a girl? Lexi... never mind. When can I see them doctor?"

"We will take you down for a short visit in just a little while, but for now, rest up. Dr. Livingston will be here first thing in the morning."

"The rest of you can come take a peek in the window, if you'd like," the doctor told them and led the way out.

"Lexi, did you buy all boy stuff?" Lyssa asked before they walked out.

"Hell yeah... How did I read it wrong?"

"Because we was high that day niece," Aunt Shirley chimed in and everyone laughed.

"We'll be right back sister," the girls said and left, followed by their mom and aunt.

"You not going with them?" Drea asked D'Mari.

"Nah babe, Ima wait and go with you." He grabbed her hand and kissed it.

"Thank you, Andrea-soon-to-be-Mitchell. You have made my life complete and I didn't know that I even had any missing puzzles. You gave me you, and now you have given me a son and a daughter. There's nothing else that I need, except solidifying our relationship and making all of the special people in my life have my last name."

Drea was crying like someone had died by the time D'Mari was done talking. She didn't know what she had done to deserve such a wonderful man, and the fact that everything resulted from a one-night stand was crazy. But, even if she could, there wasn't one thing that she would change.

"I love you, D'Mari… and I can't wait to take your last name as mine. The way we met was wild as hell, but you changed my life for the better and I can't wait to spend the rest of my days with you. Now, let's name our babies before they let me go and see them."

"I love you more, babe... you know lil man gotta be a junior, so I'll let you name the girl."

"DJ huh... well I'll name baby girl once I lay eyes on her."

A few minutes later, a nurse came in and told Drea that she was about to assist her to go and see her babies. Both D'Mari and the nurse helped her. Even though Drea was in pain, she wouldn't dare say it because she was ready to see her babies. The nurse pushed the wheelchair as they walked down the hall while D'Mari walked on the side holding Drea's hands. When they rounded the corner, Drea saw her whole family standing there. J.R. and D'Mani were there, too, along with Kyler. The only person missing was Abraham. Drea missed her dad something serious. She made it to the window and looked in on her tiny little babies.

"DJ and Ava!" Drea finally said their names and everyone smiled.

Chapter 17

A week later, Anastasia was back in New York and sitting uncomfortably in D'Mani's wraith as Kyler asked her a million questions from the back seat. They were at Dave & Buster's to meet with Zyree, but the minute they got there D'Mani told her to stay in the car while he had a few words with him. Fear gripped her as she watched them through the window, with her hand on the door handle, ready to interject if needed. They were both the type to never back down, so there was no telling what would happen.

"Ma, is that the man from grandpa funeral?" Kyler questioned, snapping Anastasia out of her thoughts.

"Uhhhhh, yeah," she told him, shocked that Zyree had even made that much of an impression for Kyler to remember him.

"Is D'Mani his friend? Is he comin inside with us?"

"Yes, and yes Kyler," she answered, never taking her eyes off of the two men. Zyree who was facing the car locked eyes with her and an amused look covered his face.

"Please lawd, don't let it be no mess,"sShe said under her breath right before D'Mani turned and started back towards the car. Anastasia tried to gauge his mood, but neither his face nor body language gave anything away.

"Come on, bae." D'Mani opened the door and helped her out of the car.

"Is everything okay?" Stasia asked, searching his face for any trace of anger or irritation. He smiled and planted a soft kiss on her lips.

"We all good, Stasia, relax," he attempted to reassure her, but she wouldn't be able to "relax" until the whole meeting was over. Anastasia could see Zyree's ass as he stood off to the side just watching them. Not wanting to give him the satisfaction of knowing she was anxious, she nodded and pecked D'Mani back.

"Don't even worry bout that nigga, I already told him what's up," D'Mani said looking back at Zyree and throwing him a head nod.

She didn't know how true that was, but she figured that if they'd been able to have a conversation without a fight maybe they could get through the rest of the evening for Kyler's sake and her sanity.

Anastasia moved over so that he could close her door and let Kyler out. It made her smile to see the two interact. She loved how close they'd gotten.

"Wassup lil dude, remember me?" Zyree asked jumping in between them with a fist out for Kyler to bump. Her attitude instantly appeared as she watched her son greet his father happily. To her surprise D'Mani remained cool, despite the intrusion.

"Let's gone inside so I can show you some of these moves." Zyree shot a smug look in D'Mani's direction, as Kyler stuck his hand in his.

"Let's go!" Kyler shouted excitedly.

They took off ahead of them as Anastasia latched on to D'Mani's arm. She could feel the tension from his shoulders on down, but he didn't let it show as they followed Zyree inside.

"Don't let his petty antics get to you," Stasia sighed.

"Oh, I'm good. Besides, I won't act a fool in front of Ky." He shrugged, holding the door open for her.

"I got plenty time to kill his ass later." He pretended to joke, but Anastasia knew he was dead ass serious.

An hour later, after she had watched both men compete in every game, they sat around the table eating burgers. The conversation flowed easily between Kyler and Zyree the same way it had at her father's repast. It was obvious that the two had a connection and for a second Anastasia almost forgot about the bullshit Zyree had been pulling lately.

"Ma, did you hear that? Zy said he can help me practice for basketball!" Kyler said loudly with a mouth full of food.

Anastasia gave Zyree an evil expression because they hadn't finalized any plans, but the excited look on their son's face melted her heart. Despite the fucked-up situation they were in, she wanted nothing more than for Kyler to enjoy his dad's company. If she could just get him to only want to be a father, and not a family then they'd be alright.

"Ohh that's cool." She gave him a tight smile.

"We just need to make sure it fits into your schedule first, ok?"

"Well, I can work around whatever he got goin on," Zyree offered once he saw Kyler's smile fade. Anastasia kicked him in his shin underneath the table and smirked at his pain.

"You don't even live here, so it wouldn't be that easy to do. We can figure that out later, but I don't mind you teaching him some things while you're in town," she suggested, taking a sip of her drink. It was obvious Zyree wanted to disagree, but that wasn't Anastasia's concern. He was being extremely presumptuous thinking to offer his time without talking to her first. If he kept that mess up, he wasn't going to have to worry about D'Mani, because she was gone kill his ass.

"Zy understands, ain't that right?" D'Mani cut in flashing his perfect teeth, just as Zyree was about to say something.

"Yeah, we can talk about it later." Zyree nodded, but it was clear that he was anything but happy about having to wait.

Anastasia wasn't sure what had been discussed outside, but whatever it was had Zyree in line and she was loving it. After that things seemed to go fine and Kyler talked to his father about all types of things like school and his friends. She knew how easy it was to talk to Zyree so she could understand her son's willingness to open up.

"So, how is it havin my homie D'Mani as a dad? I bet he's cool, huh?" Zyree asked, instantly killing the mood. Anastasia wanted to slap his ass to sleep for pulling that shit, and judging from the look on his face, he knew exactly what he was doing.

"My dad died," Kyler explained uncomfortably and looked down at his plate.

"Oh, my bad. I didn't know. Why don't we go play some more games and you can tell me all about him?"

"No, I think it's about time we go." Stasia was pissed. Zyree knew damn well that D'Mani wasn't his daddy.

"Just a few more games, Ma. Please!" Kyler perked right up. She had already started gathering her things to go but she didn't want to punish Kyler because of Zyree.

"Fine but let me talk to Mr. Zyree for a second first." She sighed giving Zyree a look and walking away from the table so that he could follow.

"Nigga, let me be real clear that if you keep playing games with my son…"

"Our, our son," he interjected as they came to a stop near the bathrooms.

"No, he's *my* son. He's been my son and he will remain my son, especially if you keep this bullshit up," she hissed angrily.

"Well, it/s not like I knew about him to be there from the beginning. Hell, if it wasn't for yo aunty, I still wouldn't know."

"Maybe that wouldn't have been such a bad thing," Anastasia muttered underneath her breath, but he heard her and took a step in her direction.

"What you say?"

"I know she ain't say for you to be all in her face like that!" D'Mani appeared out of nowhere and pushed him back a little.

"Didn't we just have a conversation, nigga? Don't be the next father that Ky loses bein hard headed," he threatened. Anastasia watched as the men sized each other up.

"I ain't come here for that, but I ain't gone keep lettin you come at me crazy, bruh! Don't let me bein a dad fool you. I'm with the shits, too."

"First of all, both of y'all need to calm the fuck down! Nobody's fighting, or killin, especially with my baby around," Anastasia finally said, glancing back at the table where Kyler was watching intently. She turned back to face the two men making sure not to step in between them. She wasn't dumb enough to try and stand in the middle of niggas exchanging words, so she reached out and touched D'Mani's arm softly.

"D'Mani, let's just go." It took him a few seconds but he finally broke eye contact with Zyree and nodded an okay her way.

"Yeah, listen to yo woman," Zyree taunted, causing D'Mani to grin like a madman.

He let Anastasia pull him away, but he made sure to point his fingers at Zyree in the shape of a gun. Just when she had thought the two had come to an understanding and that Zyree was done with the crazy shit, that had to happen. She quickly got her son and they all left, in different moods. D'Mani was mad, Kyler was confused and she was irritated as hell. She had planned on inviting him to Kyler's birthday the following week, but now she wasn't so sure it would be a good idea. The last thing she needed was him showing his ass in a room full of kids, friends and family. His behavior was beginning to give her Richard in his last days vibes and she wasn't feeling that crazy shit at all. She decided on the ride home after Kyler bombarded her with questions about him that she would let Zyree come to the party, at least for her son's happiness. Despite him acting an ass, Kyler liked him and it was all about making him happy. First though, she needed to get her man in a better mood because he was definitely on edge after that scene, and she would definitely need to butter him up to convince him to be in the same room with Zyree again without bullets flying. Anastasia definitely had her work cut out for her.

Chapter 18

Alyssa smiled as she stared at the picture of her niece and nephew while sitting at her desk. DJ and Ava were the most adorable babies she'd laid her eyes on in a while and she found herself staring at their pictures quite often. Since the birth of the twins, Alyssa's baby fever was more intense than before and she couldn't wait until it was her turn to become pregnant which was something she was more than looking forward to. Staring at the picture a moment longer, Alyssa placed her phone down on the desk focusing her attention on the folder before her. She hadn't started working on D'Mari's case yet because she was waiting on a response from Andrea, but with the graduation and the birth of the twins, Alyssa knew that the information she shared with her about the case was the last thing on Andrea's mind. So, she figured she'd handle things herself and it didn't involve her digging up dirt on her soon to be brother-in-law.

Alyssa's thoughts were interrupted when her co-worker that she was working on a case with began to ramble about an infidelity case that she was currently working on when thoughts of Corey instantly popped into her mind. She was tired of driving herself crazy about what was going on with him and the secrets he may or may not have been hiding. Without thinking twice, Alyssa asked her co-worker to follow her husband. Giving her a sideways glance, her co-worker watched as Alyssa jotted down Corey's information on a piece of paper. Alyssa reached in her purse and removed a few hundred-dollar bills from her money clip before handing the money and the paper to her. Without asking any questions, her co-worker promised that she would do her best before snatching everything out of Alyssa's hand. Clearing off her desk, Alyssa grabbed her purse and headed out of the office. She had a lunch date with her bestie that she dared not be late for because they were long overdue for some food and girl talk.

Arriving at their favorite restaurant ten minutes early, Alyssa parked in the nearest spot, killed the engine and made her way inside. As soon as she walked in, she spotted Kelly and made her way over to her. She was all smiles as she approached her bestie, but by the look on Kelly's face, Alyssa knew that she was pissed. Greeting each with a quick hug, they sat down and Kelly didn't hesitate to open fire on her.

"I just want you to know that I am pissed at the way we're starting to drift a part. I know that life gets in the way sometimes but it only takes two seconds to shoot a bitch a text or even call," Kels fussed.

"I know. I know and I apologize," Alyssa stated sincerely. "I've had a lot of shit on my plate lately with this new job and the stuff that's going on with Corey. So, forgive me for being distant, sis." She took a sip of her long island ice tea. Kelly had already ordered food and drinks for the both of them.

"Awww girl. Tell me what's going on?"

"Me and Corey fell out a while back because he didn't want to have kids but a week later, he had a change of heart and we've been trying to conceive ever since, but I had a feeling that he was keeping something from me. A few weeks ago, I heard him talking to someone on the phone about giving someone money by the end of the week. I've been trying to let Corey handle his business without getting involved but I need to know what the fuck is going on with my husband. So, I hired my co-worker to keep tabs on him," Alyssa shrugged.

"Alyssa! Do you think that was a good idea? I mean, you could have your co-worker following that man for nothing. He could be innocent."

"If he is, no harm done, but if he is hiding something, don't I have the right to know about it?"

"You do but at least give him a chance to tell you. He might've gotten into an embarrassing situation that he wants to handle on his own and doesn't want you knowing about it." Kelly sipped her mojito.

"I understand all that Kels but what's done is done."

Before Kelly could protest, their waiter arrived with the appetizers. After placing their food in front of him, he smiled and walked away.

"So, you told me about Corey. Now what's going on with your job?"

"The case I'm working on involves my family. Andrea's lawyer friend is requesting info on her fiancé and I need to find out what the hell he's up to?" She took a forkful of her stuffed mushrooms.

"Who? Your sister's boyfriend?"

"Hell naw. Her lawyer friend. I have a meeting with him in a couple of hours and there are some question I need to ask him."

"Are you allowed to do that?"

"If I need additional info that's going to help me with my case, yes but in this case, I'm trying to protect my family. My sister just had her babies and I'm not about to let some vindictive ass nigga fuck up her life because he has it out for her man," Lyssa stated.

"I hear that. So, I guess your ass is ready to be a housewife because you're definitely going to get fired behind this."

"Shit, it wouldn't be the first time." She shrugged.

The duo continued to chat as they finished their lunch. Kelly updated her on her job and how her workload had increased since she was promoted. The longer hours were taking a toll on her but being as though that was what she wanted, Kelly was making the most of it. As their lunch date came to an end, Alyssa promised to not be so distant as she hugged her friend goodbye. Jumping in her car, she brought it to life and pulled off into traffic making her way to Felix's office.

Parking in the lot in front of his office building, Alyssa put her hair in a bun before placing her glasses on her face. Even though she was there to gather information, she still wanted to be professional. She grabbed her purse, and hopped out of the car, locking the doors with the remote. Alyssa walked into the building like a boss catching the eye of every man and woman as she passed. She headed towards the elevator and stepped on before the doors closed. When she arrived at the fourth floor, Alyssa stepped off the elevator and strolled to the receptionist desk giving her the reason for her visit. The receptionist placed a call to Felix and seconds later, she was pointing Alyssa in the direction of his office which was down the hall. Stopping at the door with his name on it, Alyssa knocked on the door and when he called for her to come in, she entered his office.

"Good Afternoon, Mr. Alexander," she greeted with an extended hand.

"When the receptionist told me that I had meeting with a Miss Holiday, I assumed that I was meeting Andrea." He shook her hand before pointing at the seat in front of his desk.

"So, what is this meeting pertaining to?"

"You requested information on a D'Mari Mitchell and I had a few additional questions to ask you." Alyssa sat in the comfy office chair.

"I asked Johnathan to handle this. Why isn't he here?"

"Mr. Moore asked me to handle this case for him because you needed this handled in a timely manner and even though I'm fairly new, I'm good at my job, Mr. Alexander."

"If you're anything like your sister, I'm sure you're an over achiever when it comes to your career, but at the same time, I don't feel comfortable discussing this with Andrea's relative. You might try to warn her about the son of a bitch she's with," Felix spoke through clenched teeth and with a balled fist.

"Mr. Alexander, is the case personal for you? I can't help but notice your anger towards your suspect."

"Does that matter?"

"I think it does. On this form you filled out, you wrote that you needed information on Mr. Mitchell for business purposes and if this is not related to any legal case that you're working on, we need to know why you want this information for your personal benefit."

Felix gave her an intense stare and if Alyssa was easily intimidated, she would have folded but she didn't. She returned his stare and waited for him to respond.

"Even though I'm sure you're just doing your job, I don't think it matters if the case is business or personal. I need information on D'Mari Mitchell and since you're responsible for handling this case, you better do a damn good job of getting me every detail of his life because if you fuck this up, your ass will be doing time for protecting a criminal that is suspected of murder," Felix rose from his seat.

"Is that a threat, Mr. Alexander?" Alyssa rose to her feet as well, leaning on his desk.

"Try me and find out. I'm a well-known attorney and I know people in high places. All it takes is one phone call and I can fuck up your entire life. So, what's it going to be, Miss Holiday?"

Alyssa's blood was boiling over from Felix's threats. She wanted to cuss his ass out something awful but she decided that silence was the key at that point.

"I'll have the information you need in two weeks." She gave a devious smile leaving Felix confused.

Walking out of the office, the wheels were spinning in her head. Alyssa needed to figure out how she was going to handle the situation and fast. Gathering information on D'Mari was out of the question but thoughts of blackmailing Felix or the possibility of him coming up missing put her worries to ease. Alyssa didn't know how she was going to accomplish her mission but she was going to complete it at all cost.

Chapter 19

Alexis's heart was filled with so much joy looking at her brand-new niece and nephew. She remembered the feeling once before and that's when Kyler was born. Because she didn't have any kids of her own, she loved them with everything in her.

"Auntie will be back tomorrow DJ and AJ," Lexi cooed as she leaned over in the little cribs that would house them for the next weeks.

"AJ?" Drea repeated with a perplexed look on her face as she gathered her belongings.

"D'Mari Jr. and Alexis Jr. What the fuck you thought it stood for?" she questioned.

Unable to hold her composure, Andrea busted out in laughter. She kissed the twins goodbye before promising to return in a few hours. They had to practically drag her away from the hospital but Lexi didn't blame her, no new mother wanted to be without their babies. Although the arrival of the twins was unplanned, Alexis was still happy to have her sister in Atlanta with her a little longer. Not only could they bond, she was able to spend time with her new bundles of joy. The thought of attending grad-school in New York weighed heavily on her mind. She still hadn't told her family about the acceptance letter because she wasn't too sure of her next moves.

"So, what we got planned?" Andrea asked as she hopped in the passenger side of Lexi's car.

"WE? Bitch, I'm dropping you off to your man at the hotel. Y'all staying in and I'm going home," Lexi assured her.

"Damn, really Baby Holiday, that's how you'll do me?" Drea poked out her bottom lip but to no effect on her youngest sibling.

"Yes, you need some rest and that's what you are going to get. Now, do you need me to stop and get you something to eat before I drop you off?" Lexi questioned.

"Nah, I'm good," Drea replied, rolling her eyes and folding her arms across her chest.

Lexi laughed at how stubborn Drea was being but truth was, she did need to get some rest and that's what she was going to get.

After dropping Drea off, Lexi got a call from Marcus, who just so happened tobe in the neighborhood again. Lexi told

Marcus to meet her at the Waffle House near her place because she hadn't eaten anything all day. She pulled up, parked, killed the engine and grabbed her phone, going to the Facebook app first. Lexi noticed a red notification in the upper right-hand corner indicating she had an inbox. Clicking on the small icon, Lexi had a few unread messages but the most recent one caught her eye.

Tamika Loving My Man Wells: I don't know you and you don't know me, but I was directed to your page because we have someone in common. Apparently, J.R. has been playing the both of us, from my understanding, he's my man and judging from the pictures on your page, he's yours, too. I'm coming to you woman to woman regarding this because I don't feel like we should allow him to play us.

Lexi couldn't believe the shit she was reading. She hadn't had a bitch inbox her about a nigga since high school. Without thinking twice, Lexi wrote her back.

Sexi Lexi: J.R who?

Lexi's eyes never left her red iPhone screen as she waited for a response. She knew the bitch had to be thirsty because those three dots appeared, indicating that she was writing back only seconds after the message was sent. Lexi waited impatiently but got the shock of her life when shortly replied with a picture of J.R. laying in herbed. Just as she was about to write back, Marcus knocked on the car window, causing her to jump.

"Bring ya ass!" he yelled, before walking towards the restaurant.

Without replying, Lexi tucked her phone into her purse and got out the car. She looked up at the gray skies and began to powerwalk before it started to pour down. Once inside, she followed Marcus who followed a waitress to their booth.

"What's wrong?" Marcus asked, as soon as she slid in.

"Nothing," she lied, grabbing a menu and opening it up.

Lexi's eyes scanned over her options but she no longer had an appetite. Truthfully, she didn't know how to deal with the new information that she had just received, so she did the only thing she knew to do and that was to tell her sisters. Alexis went to the Holiday sister's group message and kicked shit off.

Lexi: Aye y'all

Lyssa: What's up?

Stasia: Sup?

Drea: Fuck you!

Lexi laughed at Drea's old stubborn ass before filling her sisters in.

Lexi: I just got an inbox from some random bitch, claiming that J.R. is her man. She even sent me a picture of him sleeping peacefully in her bed.

Stasia: Stop lying.

Lexi: I wish I was.

Alexis placed her phone down on the table when the waitress arrived to take their order. Requesting a waffle plate with turkey bacon and orange juice, she handed her menu back to the young lady and picked up her phone.

Lyssa: What's the bitch name? I'm finna look her up?

Drea: I'm on my way, drop your location.

Lexi: lol nah, it's cool y'all. Small thing to a giant but I'm out with Marcus, I'll hit y'all back when I'm done eating.

Lexi placed her phone back on the table, only to find Marcus staring at her when she lifted her head.

"What?" She smacked her lips.

"Alexis Denise Holiday. What's wrong?" he quizzed.

Lexi never hid anything from Marcus so she went ahead and spilled the beans. He too couldn't believe the shit but unlike everyone else, Lexi didn't put shit pass NO nigga. J.R. never gave her a reason to think he was unfaithful but then again, was Lexi blinded by the love so much that she didn't even pay attention to it? The two friends talked a little more before their food arrived. Lexi dug into the waffles but after the third bite, she was running off to the bathroom. She made it into the empty stall just in time to release everything that was in her into the nasty toilet bowl. Satisfied with the results and feeling slightly better, she walked out of the stall and ran directly into Marcus.

"This is the ladies room. What the fuck you doing in here?" Lexi questioned.

"No, why the fuck are you in here throwing up?" he shot back.

"Nigga, I did just eat," she replied, walking around him and to the sink.

"Bitch please… here," he said, rambling through the black Chanel bag he carried.

Lexi washed her hands and splashed some water on her face before turning back around to face him. Just as she did, Marcus pulled out a home pregnancy test and waved it in her face.

"MARCUS! WHY THE FUCK ARE YOU JUST CARRYING AROUND PREGNACY TESTS?" she yelled.

"Girl, yo pussy ain't the only one that get wet. Now, go back in there and piss on this," he instructed.

Wanting to object but knowing he would not go away that easily, she snatched the test out of his hand and did as she was told. Waiting on the results was the longest two minutes in the world. Women flowed in and out of the bathroom, turning up their noses at the presence of Marcus but they simply asked them, "what the fuck you looking at" and kept waiting. Lexi began to pace the bathroom floor when Marcus went over and grabbed the test off of the window ledge.

"OH, MY GOD!" he screamed.

"What? What? What? she rushed over and asked.

"You popped, bitch," Marcus said, handing her the test that displayed two lines, clear as day.

Lexi stared at the results, the only words she could say, finally escaped her lips.

"I KNOW YOU FUCKIN LYING!"

Chapter 20

It had been two weeks since Drea had given birth to her little bundles of joy. May 5th was a day that she would never forget. Lexi's graduation and the twin's birthday. They were still very tiny but didn't have any issues. Dr. Livingston as well as the doctor that delivered the twins wanted both of them to weigh at least five pounds before they discharged them. With the way that they were eating, it would only be a few more weeks. Drea had tried the breastfeeding thing for about three days but got so frustrated that she gave up and fed them Similac. Of course, she cried about it, but D'Mari, along with her mom assured her that the babies would still be just fine. She didn't argue after another day or so because DJ and Ava were both doing so well. One of the nurses told her that she could try again once the babies got bigger, but Drea pretty much put the thought out of her mind.

"You wanna go and get something to eat, sweetie?" Ms. Mitchell inquired.

"I'm actually kinda hungry this time," Drea smiled.

"Good... I need you to keep your strength up for them babies. And don't you be tryna overdo it, let Mari do his part.

I'm so happy I finally got me some grandbabies," Ms. Mitchell rambled on and Drea just smiled and agreed with everything that she said.

They continued talking while walking down the hall and then ran into her mom and aunt.

"Where y'all goin?" Aunt Shirley demanded to know.

"Stop being rude, auntie. We bout to go and get something to eat...I guess to the cafeteria unless y'all wanna leave the hospital."

"We can eat in the cafeteria baby... that way you can be close like I know you wanna be, but you're leaving to go and get some rest tonight," Victoria stated.

Drea decided not to argue with her mom. She would never admit it out loud, but she was really tired as hell. The need to be near her babies twenty-four seven weighed heavily on her mind and Drea just wanted to make sure they were fine. Thoughts of what she did wrong constantly plagued her mind, but the doctors assured her that she did absolutely nothing wrong and it wasn't uncommon to deliver two months early even though she was initially told a month. A phone rang just as they got on the elevator and Aunt Shirley pulled her phone from her purse and answered loud as hell. Drea was sure that the eardrums for whoever was on the other end had just burst.

"Hey baby... wait a minute I can't talk like I want to I got a bunch of nosey heifers around me," Aunt Shirley laughed and Drea wondered when in the hell she started caring about who was around.

"Ronald, baby, you gon make me leave my sister over here in Georgia and come put it on you."

Drea's eyes bucked at the revelation. She knew that had to be Ronald. The fact that he showed up at the gender reveal showed that they had really hit it off. Drea only met him briefly until things went left and she ended up going into labor. The thought of Aunt Shirley actually entertaining him never crossed Drea's mind, she just assumed that she would cuss his ass out and he would go on about his damn business. To say that she was shocked would have been an understatement. By the time they made it to the cafeteria, Aunt Shirley was off the phone and she grabbed Drea's arm.

"See, I thought I was gon have to cuss you out for giving Ronald my number, but he can lay the pipe real good. I didn't get to thank you since you had them babies right after you met him. Thank ya, suga," Aunt Shirley halfway whispered and then kissed Drea on the jaw.

Everyone knew she couldn't really whisper to save her life, but she had done a decent job just then.

"Ewww auntie... that's just too much information," Drea waved her off.

"What, you think yo auntie too old to get some... well baby I ain't. I was on a lil drought, but thanks to you I'm good and I guess I'll let you have D'Mari after all.

"Gee, thanks so much Aunt Shirley," Drea laughed.

"You know I love you, baby, but not like I love Lexi. But come to think of it, this might bump you up past her, don't tell her I said that though."

Drea rolled her eyes and kept moving forward. She knew that going back and forth with her aunt would have been like arguing with a brick wall. After they secured a table, the ladies went and fixed their plates. Drea was happy to see that her mom and Ms. Mitchell were getting along so well. Warnings of Aunt Shirley had been given in advance so all was well in that category. Drea was trying to shake back, so the only thing she fixed was a salad.

"Drea, baby, you gotta eat more than that. You've already lost most of your pregnancy weight, so don't starve yourself," Victoria scolded her after they were all seated.

"Moommm I'm gonna eat something later. D'Mari said something about going to eat at Ruth Chris so I'm sure I'll pig out. I'm not starving right now," Drea expressed.

"You mother is right… don't starve yourself. And that's all I'm gonna add. This hospital sure does have some good food though. I've always heard all of the food is better in the south and I'm starting to believe it," Ms. Mitchell chimed in.

While they ate, the women gave Drea good motherly advice, even Aunt Shirley. Of course, she was dramatic and cursing like a sailor as she talked, but everyone was accustomed to her ways and didn't expect anything less. Drea finished eating before everyone else and excused herself to the bathroom. She handled her business, washed her hands and as she exited, she felt her phone vibrate. Assuming that it was D'Mari, Drea answered without looking but got the shock of her life.

"You back, babe?"

"Actually, I am… I got word that you delivered a couple of weeks ago and I'm here to see you now."

Drea moved the phone away from her ear and looked at the screen. She couldn't believe what Felix had just said. Thoughts of the conversations that she had with her sister about him instantly popped into her head. With everything that had been going on, Drea hadn't had time to focus on Felix, but apparently it was time to set the record straight. Before she could respond, Drea looked up and locked eyes with non-other than Mr. Felix Alexander. Her blood began to boil as she thought back to how he acted in Mississippi and the things that Lyssa told her. Drea had never looked at Felix in a romantic way and she thought the feelings were mutual, but evidently, she was wrong.

"Felix… what are you doing here? And how did you even know where I was?" Drea demanded to know with her arms folded.

"Drea, I'm a lawyer just like you... there isn't anything that we can't find out if we really wanna know, right?" He smiled.

"Okay, what's the real issue here? You've changed lately and I can't say that it's for the best."

"Honestly, I've always wanted you, Drea. I should have admitted this a long time ago, but I didn't. When I came to Mississippi, I had finally gotten up enough nerves to ask you to be mine, only to find out that you were pregnant. One part of me wanted to say forget it and move on, but the other part wanted to continue to pursue you and..."

"I'm happy, Felix. I'm sorry that you developed feelings for me, but the feelings aren't mutual. I don't have just a baby daddy, I'm engaged to the father of my children and we are just fine. I would like to keep our friendship, but if you can't stay in your lane, I'll have no choice but to back away," Drea cut him off and said.

"Do you really know this man, Drea? Isn't he a thug? You're willing to marry a thug and you're an outstanding lawyer?" Felix quizzed.

"Wow Felix… so this is what we're doing? After all of these years of friendship, this is what it resulted to?" Drea shook her head.

"All I'm asking is that you give us a chance, Drea?"

"A chance to do what?" D'Mari appeared out of nowhere and wrapped his arms around Drea and pulled her close.

"Uhh… umm," Felix stuttered.

"Save it clown… if we was anywhere else besides this hospital, you would see exactly how much of a thug I really am, but today is your lucky day so I advise you to skip yo tight pants wearing ass on back out that door," D'Mari calmly, but firmly stated.

Drea watched as Felix back pedaled away and shook her head. She had to admit that she was a bit sad because she truly valued their friendship, but it was clear that it was over.

"I heard everything he said. You better tell that corny nigga to fall the fuck back," D'Mari advised her.

"I got a way to handle him. It's like he said, lawyers have a way of finding out everything."

Drea wanted to tell D'Mari about the threat that Felix had made to Lyssa, but she kept it to herself. She knew exactly how to handle the situation without violence, but if that didn't work, she wouldn't have a problem telling her fiancé to make her problem disappear.

Chapter 21

Anastasia ran around trying to put the finishing touches on Kyler's party decorations. She was probably more excited than he was. Since his favorite thing was basketball, she decided to decorate their new backyard in just that. She had about ten tables set up with a black and orange table cloth, with jerseys on the back of each chair, and a centerpiece of basketball themed balloons. Off to the side was a long table with a black and white striped tablecloth, on it she had basketball paper plates, bottles of water and Gatorade with sweatbands on them, little white baskets that looked like nets, filled with cheeseballs, and other things like chips and candy.

On each end of the table she had a balloon column stand decorated with all orange and black balloons. Anastasia didn't stop there, she had made a scoreboard to place behind the table, with Kyler's name on it too, and that was just a few of his decorations. She set the tower of cupcakes she was holding that were designed to look like little basketballs on the table and stepped back to admire her work. It looked good for her to not be a professional.

"Damn, it look good back here." D'Mani came into the backyard nodding in appreciation as he looked around. Anastasia couldn't help but to turn around cheesing. She was proud of the work she had done.

"Awww thanks, I didn't know if I was going to be able to pull it off."

"If you hadn't fired Ebony then yo ass wouldn't have had to worry," he teased, pulling her into him for a hug and kiss, but she turned her face so that he ended up kissing her cheek.

"Don't play with me, you know I don't trust anybody around my man with one of those names." She frowned, and D'Mani rolled his eyes at her dramatics. Anastasia had told him one night while they were chilling and watching Soul Food, that she didn't trust any woman named Faith or Ebony, cause they were always messing with somebody else's man. At first D'Mani thought she was joking, but she was dead ass serious and made sure to show him whenever they ran into a woman with either name. Ebony was originally the party planner for the couple, that D'Mani had hired to help Anastasia out. She had come highly recommended from one of his business associates, but the minute she heard the name Ebony, Stasia wasn't with the whole idea. Hell, all the girl did was give her ideas that she could have gotten off Pinterest. Besides that, Anastasia didn't like the way that she acted whenever D'Mani came around the two times that they'd met, so she fired her ass.

"I swear yo ass funny as hell, Stasia." D'Mani laughed at her and still managed to get in a kiss. She still pretended to have an attitude once he released her and grabbed a handful of snacks from the table.

"I'm serious nigga, and stop eating the kid's candy," she scolded. "They're gonna be here any minute."

"Them lil bad ass kids ain't gone miss this one handful," D'Mani said with a shrug just as the doorbell rang. Anastasia rolled her eyes and went to get it while he continued to pick at the spread of snacks on the table.

The first guests to arrive were Kyler's best friends, Joey and Brent. Since he was in one of the best private schools in the area, he had a lot of white friends that he hung out with. Anastasia loved the fact that Kyler could fit in, in any setting. She invited the boys in and led them to the backyard but had to turn right back around due to someone else being at the door. It was five more kids and she directed them all to where the other boys were.

Before she knew it, she had at least twenty kids running around her house and yard while their parents sat on the patio furniture and drank mimosas. It had only been about a half hour and Anastasia was ready to sit down and do the same thing. Her phone rang in her pocket and she took it out to see that Drea and Lexi were FaceTiming her.

"Hey y'all." She cheesed once she was in the kitchen and away from the loud party.

"Where my nephew at? Ain't nobody called to talk to youl" Lexi was the first to speak.

"Hi Stasia," Drea said with a laugh.

"Whateva hoe, but he stayed with Lyssa and Corey last night, they should be bringing him in a second. Hey Drea, how are my niece and nephew?" Stasia gushed. Even though her and her sisters talked more frequently she was still excited to see the twins, like any new Aunt.

"*My* niece and nephew, you know I'm their favorite aunt." Both Anastasia and Drea laughed at Lexi being a brat, before Drea turned the camera on the twins who were both in what appeared to be dressed in a pink and blue onesie, with little hats on.

"Awwww they're so cute!" Anastasia cooed. The twins were giving her baby fever, from how adorable they were, but she wasn't ready to have any more kids, or risk having twins since it obviously ran in D'Mani's family.

"Girl, they're cute right now while they're sleep. Let them get hungry and that cuteness goes away fast!" Drea joked.

"Aye! Stop talkin bout my kids, Drea!" D'Mari yelled from somewhere in the background and caused all of the sisters to chuckle.

"Yeah bitch, stop talkin bout my niece and nephew like I won't come over there." Lexi threatened. "And why don't they have on the outfits I brought you?"

"Cause they're not goin anywhere right now, Baby Holiday," Drea sighed into the phone and flipped the camera back around to her face. Anastasia could tell that her big sister was tired, and she was glad that D'Mari and Lexi were around to help her out with the twins.

"Well, I'm bouta come dress them, they need to be photoshoot ready at all times. My lil diva can't be just layin around in a onesie!" Lexi fussed with a frown, causing Drea to roll her eyes.

"Okay, but be prepared to fight D'Mari, I'ma go to sleep on both y'all ass."

"Girl, I ain't scared, he don't wanna get in the middle of an Auntie and her babies!"

Anastasia giggled as the two went back and forth, glad that her and her sisters were in such a good place with each other. It seemed like it had been years since they were constantly fighting each other and now they got along way better.

"I'm not bouta argue with you, Lexi. Come on to the hospital if you comin," Drea finally said and ended the bickering.

"You already knew I was comin, but is yo retarded ass baby daddy comin to my nephew party, Stasia?" Lexi questioned now that they had come to an agreement. Honestly, Anastasia hadn't thought too much about whether or not Zyree would come to the party. She had been ignoring him since the disaster at Dave & Buster's, but she had still sent him an invite. There was no doubt though that he would bring his ass, she just hoped he didn't act a damn fool when he got there.

"I don't really know, I did invite him though," she sighed and grabbed some more of the Gatorade she had out of the fridge, since she was sure the kids had run through the ones that she had out there.

"Hmph, he better not get on no crazy shit or I'ma have to take a flight!" Lexi threatened and Anastasia already knew that she was serious about doing so.

"Well, I hope he don't, poor Kyler has been through enough, but I sent him some games and clothes for his birthday. They should be there today if you haven't got them already," Drea chimed in.

"And my gift is a surprise, but it should be there today, too. But, I'm bouta go get dressed so I can go see the babies."

"Okay, I'll have D'Mari come unlock the door for you."

"Bitch, I got a key already!" Lexi laughed. "Bye y'all."

"Bye."

"Heffa," Drea chuckled with an eye roll. "Bye Stasia," she said and disconnected the call. Anastasia could only imagine what Drea was going through living so close to Alexis with those babies. She was going to have to go see them again soon before she tried to turn the kids against her. The doorbell rang again and Anastasia looked at her watch to see that it was going on two in the afternoon. She peeked out to see Kyler, Lyssa and Corey all holding a bunch of bags. Without trying to make too much noise, she hurried to the backyard to tell everybody to get ready to surprise him and then went to open the door for the birthday boy.

As soon as she swung the door open her good mood disappeared at the sight of Zyree standing next to her son with a gift bag and balloons in each hand. He gave her a sneaky ass smirk as Kyler ran in and hugged her.

"Sup Stasia, where you want me to sit this?" he asked like their last encounter wasn't a bad one. She shared a look with her sister and noticed that Corey was staring at Zyree with a frown. It was obvious that D'Mani had filled him in on what had been going on with Zyree.

"Look who I saw, Ma!" Kyler said and jumped up and down. She wanted to be as enthusiastic as her son about his father coming, but she just couldn't. The look in his eyes had told her that he would get on some straight bullshit and she wasn't trying to have that at her son's party.

"I see, well let's go in the back so I can show you what I got for your birthday." She forced a smile on her face and took ahold of Kyler's hand.

"Hey Stasia." Lyssa stepped inside with Corey right on her heels.

"Hey sis, where my cousin?" he asked looking at Zyree still.

"Wassup y'all, he's out back though, come on." Stasia led the small group through the house without acknowledging Zyree and into the backyard. She was surprised to see that all of the kids and grownups had hidden well, because it looked vacant besides the decorations.

"Dang Mama this is cool!" Kyler said loudly and at the sound of his voice all of his guests jumped out of hiding and yelled out "Happy Birthday." He was so surprised that he almost ran back into the house and had everybody laughing. D'Mani came up before any of his friends could reach him and slapped hands with him.

"Wassup lil man, happy birthday."

"Thanks D! Did you see I brought your friend with me, and he got presents?" Kyler pointed back at Zy and Stasia could see him flex his jaw, before he put on a fake smile like she had.

"Oh, that's wassup, why don't you go hang out with yo friends and I'ma keep Zy company," he told him and nodded towards the group of kids that were running around. Kyler didn't even say anything, he just took off and D'Mani walked over to put his arm around Anastasia, with his eyes still on Zyree.

"If you want him to leave, I'll get this nigga outta here," was all he said.

"No, no it's okay, Zyree's gonna be cool," Stasia stuttered and placed a calming hand on his chest.

"I ain't on shit, but what I been on, and that's getting to know my son. All that other shit is for another time and place," Zyree just had to comment, before he walked off to join Kyler and play.

"Watch what I tell you I'ma have to kill that nigga," D'Mani threatened, finally giving Anastasia his attention.

"I was thinkin the same shit cuz," Corey said, bumping fists with his cousin.

"Well, let's hope it doesn't get that far," Alyssa mumbled. Her and Anastasia both knew what their men were capable of, but they still didn't like it.

"Come on, let's just enjoy the party y'all. We can talk about this later." Anastasia didn't want to think about her son having to lose another father due to their crazy behavior, but she also knew that if Zyree kept it up there would be bloodshed. She managed to get D'Mani to loosen up and the rest of the party went off without a hitch thankfully.

Later after all the guests had left and Kyler had finally settled down, Anastasia got ready to read him a bedtime story. She got onto his bed and got comfortable.

"Did you have fun today?" she asked him as he rubbed at his eyes sleepily.

"Yeah, it was a lot of fun, and I loved my presents, specially from Auntie Drea and Auntie Lexi!" Lexi's gift had definitely been a surprise, her crazy ass had sent him a little dirt bike like Anastasia would ever let him ride such a thing. She was already thinking of ways to distract him from wanting to get on that thing.

"Yeah, I liked that, too," she lied. "Did you like having Zyree over?" She wanted to know, hoping that he hadn't said anything too forward to their son.

"Aww yeah, all my friends wanted to sign up for his basketball team he said he's making."

"Well, I don't know about that Kyler, he lives pretty far away, so that may be awhile," Stasia said with a frown. She didn't know why he would get Kyler's hopes up about that shit knowing that he still lived in Mississippi.

"No, he doesn't, his house is down the street," Kyler yawned. Anastasia thought she had heard him wrong, but when she asked him to repeat himself it was exactly what she had heard the first time. Zyree's crazy ass had moved into her

neighborhood without even telling her.

Chapter 22

Between the meeting with Felix and waiting for her co-worker to dig up dirt on her husband, Alyssa was relieved when Memorial Day rolled around. It gave her a chance to relax and forget about the stress of her job and whatever her husband was hiding. Even if it was just for the day. Alyssa had plans to stay in and chill with her husband but when her co-worker invited them to a cookout she was having that day, Alyssa figured they would slide through and see what it was hitting for. Although her co-worker stressed that she didn't have to bring anything, Alyssa prepared seafood salad and grabbed two bottles of wine from Wine and Spirits the night before.

As she waited for Corey to finish getting dressed, Alyssa fixed a small plate of her dish to make sure it tasted right. After tasting a forkful, she nodded her head in approval before taking another bite.

"You ready, bae?" Corey strolled in the kitchen with his keys in hand.

"Mmm hmm but taste this first," she stuffed the fork in his mouth.

"That's good as fuck," he took the plate from her finishing off the rest of the seafood salad.

Alyssa shook her head at Corey and smiled before she placed a lid on the container and placed it in a bag. Corey grabbed the bag that had the two bottles of wine in it and they headed out the door. When Corey unlocked the doors to his car, he held the door open for her while she slid in the passenger seat. After closing her door, she watched him as he jogged around to the other side of the car, hopped in, crunk up the car and pulled off. As Alyssa navigated Corey to Elaine, her co-worker's house, she gave her husband the side eye as he drove. Feeling her eyes on him, Corey glanced in her direction before stopping at a red light.

"Wassup?" he questioned.

"That's what I'm trying to figure out."

"What the hell are you talkin' about, Lyssa?"

"Why the hell are you so happy?"

"Since we started workin' we haven't really been able to do no couple shit in a while. When I come home from work, you're either sleep or I be the fuck tired. I'm happy because I actually get to spend some real time with you and I get to meet ya co-workers and shit, which I'm actually lookin' forward to." He smiled, placing his hand on her thigh.

After hearing Corey's response to her question, Alyssa was all smiles. A part of her wanted to say that he was full of shit but being as though he had a point about them not spending that much time together, she accepted his answer and eased up a little bit. They made small talk about the family and their jobs until they arrived at their destination thirty minutes later. Elaine lived in Valley Stream, NY, which was known to be the best place to live in the state of New York. Killing the engine, Corey hopped out and opened the door for her before grabbing the bottles of wine from the back seat. Alyssa admired the house for a few seconds before Corey grabbed her by the hand guiding her to the backyard where they heard laughter and saw the smoke from the grill. Alyssa was surprised to see most of her co-workers there with their kids and spouses. Even though she'd been working there for a few months, neither of them discussed their personal lives at the office. So, it was going to be interesting to see how they got along outside of work.

Spotting Elaine over by the grill, the couple made their way over to her. Alyssa said a silent prayer that she would play like she hadn't seen her husband before. Elaine was still gathering information on her husband and Alyssa didn't want her to slip up. When they reached her, Alyssa tapped her on the shoulder getting her attention.

"Hey Alyssa! I'm glad you could make it to my little get together," Elaine gave her a quick hug. "And who might this be?" She locked eyes with Corey.

"Elaine, this is my husband Corey. Corey, this is one of my co-worker's, Elaine. We worked a case together a few weeks back."

"Well, it's nice to you meet you and welcome to my home," Elaine smiled.

"Thank you and same here." He gave her a head nod.

"Where do you want me to put this?" Alyssa held up her container.

"Your ass is hard headed. I told you that you didn't have to bring anything," Elaine fussed.

"Look, I'm from the South and when you're visiting someone's home for the first time, you bring a gift, damn it," Alyssa scolded. "Now, where do you want me to put this?"

"Over there on the table. I wish the rest of these motherfuckers woulda brought something. This is my third year inviting them to my cookouts and they always show up empty handed," Elaine shook her head. "But, go head and make yourselves at home."

"Aight." They walked over to the table where the rest of the side dishes and drinks were.

"Elaine seems cool," Corey chuckled.

"A little too cool. Until now, I never heard her cuss before. I guess people really do act different outside of work, huh?" They shared a laugh.

After placing everything on the table, Alyssa walked around the yard introducing her husband to the rest of her co-workers. About an hour later, Corey and the rest of the men were standing in a circle discussing sports while the women chilled with Elaine by the grill with cups of wine in their hands. They were having a good time laughing and drinking until Elaine expression changed.

"Aww shit. Your boo just showed up, Alyssa," Elaine smirked.

"My boo is already here."

"Not Corey. I'm talking about your work husband," Elaine chuckled.

Alyssa looked behind her and saw Johnathan shaking hands with the men. She found herself staring at her boss a little longer than she was supposed to but he looked even better than usual in his street clothes.

"Alyssa, you better stop staring at Johnathan like that before your nigga whoop your ass out here. It's cool when y'all are at work but not in front of your husband." Trish, the receptionist, shook her head.

"I didn't think y'all paid attention to us like that," Alyssa whispered.

"Girl please. I've been working for that nigga for three years and not once has he complimented me on my outfits, brought me breakfast and coffee or asked me to work a case with him," Elaine pointed out.

"Wait a minute. I thought everyone worked their first case with Johnathan." Alyssa looked between Elaine and Trish.

"Fuck no. After I was hired, his ass handed me my case and sent me on my way. He did the same thing with the guys, too. You're the only one he baby stepped into this business and he's been flirting with you ever since," Elaine added.

Alyssa downed the rest of her drink before walking over to the table and pouring a couple of shots of vodka before throwing them back. She let Elaine's words sink in and everything that she said made sense to her. After their case was over, Johnathan would bring her breakfast and coffee a few times and he always seemed to go out of his way to pay her compliments. Alyssa wondered why out of all the employees that were better qualified to work this special case for him, Johnathan chose her instead and now she knew the reason. She couldn't deny that he was sexy as fuck but other than the thoughts in her head, she never gave him a reason to believe that she was interested in him. Deep in thought, the smell of

Johnathan's cologne quickly brought her back to reality causing her to turn around and face him.

"Hey Alyssa," he greeted with a smile.

"Hey Johnathan." She nodded.

"You're looking beautiful as usual." Johnathan eyed her up and down.

"Thank you." Alyssa gave a small smile.

They stared at each for a few seconds before she walked off.

"I understand we can't act like we usually do because your man is here but no worries, I won't tell him about us., Johnathan spoke, stopping Alyssa in her tracks as she passed.

"What do you mean you won't tell my husband about us?" she questioned with a raised eyebrow.

"The affair we're having. Do you think I pay you compliments and buy you breakfast for nothing? Why do you think everyone at the office calls us work husband and wife," he smirked.

"I don't give a fuck about what you think we got going on or what the office calls us because at the end of the day, I'm a happily married woman and that's all that matters."

"And on that note, my wife will not be returnin' to work. Friday was officially her last day and if you have a problem with that, then we can settle it right here, my G." Corey stood by her side staring at Johnathan intensely.

Johnathan's eyes shifted back between her and Corey and when he raised his hands in surrender, Corey grabbed her hand and they left the cookout. Opening the door for her, Corey waited for her to get comfortable before closing it and taking his place behind the wheel. As he pulled off, Alyssa tried to read her husband but she couldn't. She wanted to assume that Corey was cool but decided to make sure. Before Alyssa could speak, he beat her to the punch.

"One of the guys told me about you and Johnathan's office relationship and the only reason why I didn't go off on you back there is because he told me that you weren't sending off any mixed signals to that nigga. He said that he had a thing for you since you started workin' there but what I want to know is why you ain't tell me this nigga was crushin' on you like this," Corey spoke in a calm tone.

"To be honest Corey, I really didn't know that he was feeling me until Elaine pointed it out to me when Johnathan arrived. He would buy me breakfast and give me compliments but I thought he was just being nice. I didn't think he meant anything by it. I just found out that they called us work husband and wife." Alyssa shrugged.

"So, you didn't flirt with this nigga in any way?"

"Hell no. There's not really anytime for us to flirt with each other because I'm hardly at the office. I'm always in the field working."

Corey stared at her for a few seconds before putting his focus back on the road.

"Aight Alyssa. I believe you and as far as you workin', you don't have to worry about that shit right now. I'm makin' good money and I can hold us down. I know you still got some bread saved up from when you were an agent. So, you should be aight for now. You already know I got you if you need anythin'."

"I know you do baby and I love you so much." Alyssa gave him a quick peck on the lips.

As they held hands, Alyssa stared out the window as she thought about Johnathan. She silently thanked God that she kept to herself and decided not to act on her lustful thoughts. Alyssa never stopped to think about if Johnathan was feeling her. She just assumed that he had a chick just by how fine he was. Besides the bullshit with Johnathan, Alyssa tried to figure out what she was going to do about the case she was working for Felix. Being as though she was no longer a PI, the case was no longer her problem but the shit with Felix was never about business, it was always personal and now that she had nothing but time on her hands, Alyssa wouldn't rest until she got the tea on Felix Alexander.

Chapter 23

Drea couldn't believe it had been a whole month since she had given birth to her beautiful babies. She looked at them in awe every single day. Both of them were finally weighing in at a little over five pounds and they were healthy as can be, which meant they could finally leave the hospital. Drea was a little skeptical about the drive back to Mississippi, but she had just been praying that the twins would sleep most, if not all of the way. Drea's phone vibrated and she grabbed it and saw that she had a text from D'Mari letting her know that he was pulling up at the front door. She alerted the nurse, but deep down it would be a lie if she said that she didn't feel some type of way.

"What's wrong, sister?" Lexi looked up from her phone and asked.

"Lexi... tell me if I'm crazy, but I'm feeling some type of way about how D'Mari been back and forth to New York these past two weeks like we don't have two whole babies here," Drea vented.

"I ain't gon lie... I was wondering the same thang, but Drea you know he got businesses and shit to run. That's probably all it was, him making money. Don't go getting all depressed and shit aight," Lexi replied.

"He coulda handled that shit in advance don't ya think, but Ima just suck it up. Everything been going so good. It feels like it's almost too good to be true, ya know?"

"Dreeaaa stop tryna act like me. You and Mari good. Y'all got the babies, and now y'all bout to be married. I know that's backwards for yo perfect ass, but shit still worked out how it's supposed to." Lexi shrugged.

"Okay Baby Holiday… you got a point. I'm sure I'm just overthinking."

"Of course, I'm right. Now, let's get outta here. I'ma miss y'all when y'all leave. Let me see if they can keep the babies a little longer so y'all can stay." Lexi pouted.

"I knoowww… I'ma miss you too, sister, but we will make sure it's not too long before I make you come to visit. I would say before I come back, but I don't know how that's gon work with two little ones," Drea confessed.

They made their way down to the nurses who had DJ and Ava ready to go. They were both dressed so cute in outfits that Lexi had custom made.

"I can't wait til you have a baby," Drea told her as she took more pictures of her niece and nephew.

"Bitch… I'm too young for all that so don't try to jinx me shit," Lexi snapped.

"Well, it'll be better to have some young and not wait as long as I did," Drea advised her baby sister.

"Whatever girl. That's J.R. that want kids, not Sexi Lexi. She got a lot of more living to do before any babies' popping outta her pussy," she said and twerked, making the nurses laugh.

"Please ignore her. Our mama dropped her on the head as a baby," Drea joked with the nurses.

"Have y'all made up? What he say about the picture?" Drea quizzed.

"I still ain't said shit. Fuck J.R. I'm just playing the role until I figure some shit out," Lexi said.

"Lord, Lexi…"

"I got this," Lexi cut her off and Drea sighed.

Drea and Lexi followed the nurses as they made their way to the elevator. A little exhaustion came upon Drea and she said a silent prayer that the babies would sleep the whole way to Mississippi because she could see herself doing just that. Her mom and aunt had left the day before and Drea knew that her mom had been to her house and cleaned from top to bottom, even though it was already clean. Drea knew that her and D'Mari were going to have to talk about their situation soon. They had been talking about it, but thought they would have a little more time before they had to make a drastic change. As soon as they made it outside, D'Mari was at the entrance smiling and waiting. His smile made butterflies form in Drea's heart. All of the feelings she had moments ago left just that quick. He was standing in front of a brand-new charcoal grey Mercedes Benz GLS- Class. Drea had mentioned the SUV to D'Mari a few months back, but she never expected him to buy one. She knew for sure it wasn't a damn rental.

"Oh, my God… you didn't?" Drea squealed when she got close.

"Anything for my family." He kissed her and then started helping get the babies situated.

"Where my new truck at J.R.?" Lexi quizzed after he walked up.

"It's called HS4 ... that's where," he replied.

"See Drea... and you think I'm having some kids for this nigga." Lexi rolled her eyes.

Everyone laughed at her dramatic ass. After the babies were situated, Drea hugged Lexi and J.R. and then climbed in between the two car seats and got as comfortable as possible. She felt like it would be easier to manage from that position. D'Mari pulled away and Drea looked between her babies and smiled. Ava had gone back to sleep right away while DJ sat there and smiling and looking up. Drea made baby talk with him for a few minutes and then he drifted back off to sleep. D'Mari had been on a phone call and Drea knew that he had to be talking to his brother by the way the conversation went. He hung up right after she was done playing with DJ.

"You hungry, babe?" he asked.

"Umm.. nah not yet. I'm a little tired so I think I'm gonna try to get a nap while they are."

"Okay, but first I gotta let you know that something came up," Mari said and Drea became alarmed. She knew there was about to be some bad news.

"I gotta hop on a flight ASAP to hop on some shit so I can either drive y'all to Mississippi and fly from Jackson or if you don't mind I can fly from here in Atlanta."

"D'Mari Mitchell are you fucking serious right now?" Drea screamed and Ava began crying immediately after her outburst.

"I'm sorry, baby." Drea rubbed her stomach and put her pacifier in her mouth.

"It's not my fault, Drea… you know how shit can go at times."

"You know what… drive to the airport here and get out. I'll get Lexi to ride with me home," Drea said pissed the fuck off.

She grabbed her phone and went to the Holiday Sister's group chat.

Drea: Y'all not gone believe this shit!!

Lexi: What's wrong?

Lyssa: What happened?

Drea: This nigga really just asked me to drop him off at the airport so he can fly to New York. RIGHT NOW!!!

Lexi: I KNOW YOU FUCKIN LYING!!!

Stasia: GTFOH!!

Drea: For real... Lexi can you ride wit me to Mississippi and I'll fly you back?

Lyssa: Wow! What the hell wrong wit Mari?

Lexi: I'm finna beat J.R. ass... we headed to somebody house and he saying it's important and won't turn the fuck around.

Stasia: So, we gotta whoop D'Mari and J.R. asses?

Drea: Ugh... I'm just ready to get away from him right now.

Lexi: Ima ride wit you Drea... as soon as this nigga park, Ima hop in the driver's seat and I'll call you.

D'mari tried to talk to Drea, but she purposely ignored him. She felt like that would be the best thing to do to keep from saying anything that she might regret in the long run. She scrolled through her social media accounts and finally posted a picture of the babies. Drea had initially said that she wasn't going to be post them until they were about a month old, but they were two weeks old and doing great so she gave in. At least she didn't post them when they were fresh out the twat like some women did.

The vehicle came to a stop and Drea assumed that they were at the airport and her anger returned. When she looked up, they were at a house and she saw Lexi standing outside fussing with J.R. When Lexi looked up, she started walking towards the truck and it was clear that she was fussing at D'Mari.

"You got my sister fucked up!" She fussed as she snatched the door open.

"Welcome to our new home, baby," Mari said and ignored Lexi.

"Huh?" Drea quizzed.

"All of the running around I been doing, it was getting this house built for us. I know you said you don't wanna rasie kids in the city, and I don't wanna move to Mississippi, so I figured this was the next best thing. You mentioned Georgia and this was the best place and we both are making sacrifices. I love you Andrea and I am going to be in my kids' lives, full time. I'm sorry for making you mad saying I was leaving, but it was only so I can see the smile on your face when you walk inside."

By the time Mari was done talking, Drea had tears streaming nonstop down her face.

"Awww Mari you so sweet. I thought I was gon have to fuck you up. Drea you got me mad at this man for nothing. Yo emotional ass gotta calm down," Lexi fussed.

"Nah sis… it's my fault. I pissed her off on purpose for real."

"Lexi, I told you to calm down," J.R. chimed in.

"Wait… you knew about this? Why you ain't tell me?" Lexi fussed at her man.

"Because you wasn't gon do shit but put it in that group chat shit," he told her.

"Thank you, baby. I love you and I appreciate you," Drea finally answered, but her tears never stopped.

"Wait… so this means that you moving to Georgia?"

"Yes Lexi," Drea laughed.

"Yeesss… wait. Well never mind. We'll talk about that later," Lexi said in a sadder than normal voice.

The house was so beautiful on the outside, Drea just knew that the inside was going to be breathtakingly gorgeous. Mari and J.R. grabbed the babies while Drea and Lexi grabbed the bags that they had and made their way inside. When they made it to the door, Drea stopped because she figured that it was locked. When Mari told her that it was unlocked, she heard Aunt Shirley's voice and turned the knob.

"Bout time y'all asses made it. I don't like how y'all keeping secrets from me. I wasn't gon tell Drea she was getting a house here."

"I thought y'all went home yesterday," Drea said.

"No baby… we wanted to stay and make sure you got settled in. This place is beautiful," Victoria said.

"Oh, my God… y'all know I'm too emotional for all of this right now," Drea sobbed.

As she walked through the house, everything that she needed was already there. The babies room was setup like a page from a magazine, the master suite was to die for and every other room was nice as hell. The five bedroom, four and half bathroom home was stunning. Drea couldn't be happier. D'Mari had once again went above and beyond to make sure that she was straight. Even though she was an independent woman, he showed her what it was like to have a real man by her side.

"How can I ever repay you?" she asked as they stood in the middle of their new bedroom?"

"Just be my wife and stay by my side through thick and thin. That's all I ask."

"You got it, Mr. Mitchell," she replied and kissed him.

"Oh, and once your six weeks are up, we gotta Christen every room in this house."

"Your wish is my command." Drea smirked and they headed back to the living room where everyone was. Drea couldn't wait to FaceTime Lyssa, Stasia, and Hannah to show them the good news. Texting wouldn't suffice.

Chapter 24

"I can't believe you aint said nothing to that man yet?" Marcus looked over from the driver seat at Lexi and stated.

"You can't believe what?" she replied, rolling her eyes and directing her attention at the cars passing by.

"Girl, don't act stupid. Not only haven't you spoken a word about the girl inboxing you to J.R., you haven't told that man you were pregnant either," he hissed.

"I ain't tell him about shorty YET, but trust, I will. I gotta get my lick back first." Lexi plotted.

"Lick back? You playing with fire, Lexi," Marcus advised her.

"Am I?" she questioned, turning around in her seat, facing him completely.

"Yes, you my girl and I'll choke a brick for you, but you wrong."

"No, the fuck I'm not. I'm not having kids by a nigga who can't keep his hoes in check."

"So, sneaking and getting this abortion is the best thing?" He quizzed as he looked through the rearview mirror suspiciously.

Realizing something felt off, Lexi turned around, catching a glimpse of the car behind her. Not recognizing it, she turned back around and focused on the conversation she was having with her best friend who turned in the parking lot of the abortion clinic.

"Look friend I just want you to rethink this, ok?" Marcus pleaded with her but his pleads fell on deaths ears.

There was nothing no one could say to talk her out of it. She had her mind made up and she refused to have kids, regardless of how much she loved a man. Without replying to Marcus, Lexi unbuckled her seatbelt, grabbed her purse from the backseat and jumped out. She adjusted the band on the Nike jogging pants she was wearing and hiked it to the front door. She stopped at the red light, allowing Marcus time to catch up with her but as soon as the light changed green, she continued her strut. Once Alexis made it inside the clinic, she glanced at the awaiting women and their supportive spouses, the small three tvs on the wall and headed to the front desk.

"Alexis Holiday, I have an appointment." She walked up and introduced herself.

Most women would be ashamed of being there but Lexi was wearing that shit like a badge of honor. After the young Latino woman searched the system, she asked for Lexi's ID and then handed her a clipboard with a stack of papers attached. Lexi happily accepted the documents before turning around and searching for Marcus who she found sitting across from a man. She headed over there towards him, thinking about what she wanted to eat when she left there.

"What's wrong with you?" she walked up and asked, noticing the weird look on Marcus's face.

"Nah, what the fuck wrong with you?" Lexi heard a voice say from behind her.

Slightly startled, she turned around and noticed J.R. standing to his feet. It was at that very moment, she had no idea of what to say or do. What was he doing there? How did he know? All the questions plagued her mind until she discovered the reason.

"I'm sorry, friend. I had to tell him," Marcus whispered, as he sat in the same spot.

"I can't believe you," Lexi snapped, cutting her eyes at him.

"Nah shorty, I can't believe you," J.R. repeated with hurt in his voice.

For the first time, Lexi felt bad but that feeling was shortly lived when she remembered the message from baby girl on Facebook.

"Well you shouldn't, especially when you been laid up with some bitch," she barked.

"Laid up with who?" he questioned as he looked at her like she lost her mind.

"This bitch…." Lexi replied before finding her phone in her purse and going to the picture she saved.

J.R. leaned forward and glanced at the photo before looking up at Lexi again confused.

"Man, that motherfuckin picture so damn old, Alexis," he laughed.

"Old my ass," she shouted, causing everyone to eye them.

"Man, shut the fuck up and look. I got dreads on here. You ain't never been with me when I had dreads," he pointed out.

For the first time in a longtime, Lexi felt dumb. She was too upset to even notice his hair. All she seen was the face and tattoos, which was enough to confirm things.

\ "So, you here, finna abort my seed over some goofy shit?" he questioned.

"I – mean—I," she stuttered.

"Man, come on," he barked, snatching the clipboard out of her hands and tossing it on the seat.

J.R. then grabbed Lexi by the hand, pulling her out while Marcus followed.

"Good looking big dog," J.R. said to Marcus who quietly went to his car.

Lexi wanted to apologize to Marcus for even being mad at him in the first place. She had placed him in a fucked-up situation. She overreacted and almost did something that she would regret later down the line. Once inside the car, Lexi sat on the passenger's side with her arms folded across her chest. She had mixed emotions about the entire situation. No J.R. might not have cheated on her, but she still felt the same way he once did about having a baby, she did not want one.

"What you want to eat?" J.R. finally asked, breaking the silence that had taken over the car for the past ten minutes.

"I'm not hungry," she lied, picking up her phone and scrolling through her apps.

"Lexi, you really were about to kill my seed?" he asked, completely switching the subject.

"I don't want no kids," she answered honestly.

"And why not?" He shot her a looked briefly before looking back at the road.

"Because I don't... DAMN!" she shot back, never looking up from her phone.

"You know what, you are so fuckn selfish man!" he snapped, snatching her phone out of her hand.

"Give me my shit." She screamed, reaching for her phone as he tried to control her and the wheel.

J.R. balanced the best way he could but unfortunately, he didn't realize he was running a red light. Before he could hit the brakes, it was too late. His all white Jeep Cherokee had crashed into a U-Haul truck that was making a right turn. Alexis was too busy trying to get her phone back to notice. The last thing she remembered was colliding with the airbags before everything went pitch black.

Chapter 25

It had been a couple of weeks, and Anastasia had calmed down about the whole Zyree moving literally two houses down from them. Of course, she'd told D'Mani about it and how weird it was, but he let her know that Zyree wasn't crazy enough to do anything stupid. In his opinion, him moving so close was just a tactic to get closer to Kyler. Him not being too worried about it made her not worry about it, and she eventually relaxed enough to allow him to start taking Kyler to his little basketball training camp, along with a few other mother's in the neighborhood, and Kyler's two best friends. Anastasia had gotten to know a few of her neighbors and Zyree had been the topic of all of their conversations. All the women thought he was handsome and were constantly trying to figure him out. She could understand their curiosity, because Zyree definitely had the mysterious thing going for him, not to mention he wasn't too bad looking either. The kids were always raving about him so were their mother's, married or divorced, all had eyes for him. She hoped that maybe, with all of the attention he would let go of this fantasy he had about getting his "family" back, like he ever had them to begin with. Although, he wasn't messaging her often, he was still messaging her shit he knew he shouldn't have been.

Anastasia kept in consideration how good he was getting along with their son, and how he'd stepped up, every time she even thought about telling D'Mani. As far as he was concerned, Zyree had let that shit go, but that was far from the truth. If D'Mani found out that he was still messaging her about anything other than Kyler he was going to kill him. The two men didn't get along at all, and damn near every time they were in each other's presence she had to referee. Zyree never took well to being told what to do, and he was always egging D'Mani on as if he wanted to see how far he could push him. Anastasia didn't know what he thought, but if kept it up D'Mani was going to lose the little bit of patience he had left. She was relieved that he hadn't made it home yet, because Kyler still hadn't gotten there and he had a set time on when he was supposed to come back. Zyree had yet to call or text and he was more than an hour late. Glancing at her watch, she realized that only a minute had passed since she last checked, so she went back to pacing back and forth in front of the large bay window in her living room. Anastasia didn't want to jump to conclusions, because Zyree had been doing a great job of bringing Kyler home, but after having Richard kidnap her baby, she couldn't put anything past anyone.

With a sigh she sent another text to his phone asking where he was, and instantly got pissed. His read receipts were on so she knew he had seen the message but was just choosing not to respond. The sound of a car pulling into her driveway, made her hurry to the front door to see Zyree's sorry ass as he got out and leisurely opened the back door for Kyler. Without thinking, she ran down the stairs barefoot and grabbed him up into a big bear hug. When she finally released him and looked into his face she could tell that he was a little upset.

"What's wrong? You okay?" she questioned and openly checked him for any visible wounds. Kyler silently looked back where Zyree stood.

"Nothing, I'm just tired." He shrugged once he faced her. Anastasia shot a nasty look at Zyree before she directed Kyler to go inside. He had barely closed the door when she jumped to her feet and was in Zy's face ready for war.

"Why the fuck are you so damn late and why is my son lookin like that? If you touched him I swear to God you'll never be able to use those fingers again!" she fussed, pointing a finger at him. The nigga had the nerve to chuckle like she was a joke. She wished that D'Mani was there because she would have let him kill his ass in their driveway.

"Mannnn ain't shit wrong with him, he said he was tired, didn't he? Damn!"

Anastasia knew he was lying through his teeth, and she wanted to punch them right down his throat. He closed the small space between them and looked down at her lustfully. "Maybe he's mad cause his mama and daddy ain't together how they should be and he need a real man around the house." Stasia scoffed and pushed him away from her with an eye roll.

"He don't even know you're his daddy, and trust me, my man takes very good care of the both of us." She wasn't in the mood for this bullshit with him and she was seriously going to consider all of Zyree's visits being supervised. "Next time you bring him home late it's really gone be a problem."

"Fuck that nigga!" His face balled up with anger.

"I plan to! She smirked. "Take yo ass home, Zy." She gave him her back and made her way to her house. It took him a few minutes but he finally pulled off and Anastasia sighed deeply. As tough as she had just pretended to be, Zyree made her nervous. He was beginning to make her uncomfortable. She finally turned away from the window to see Kyler standing there waiting.

Anastasia got down to his level and cupped his small face in her hand. "Kyler, if Mr. Zyree said or did anything that you didn't like, you can tell me."

"He didn't do anything... buuuut when we were eating he said that I was his son," Kyler told her looking extremely uncomfortable. Anastasia was shocked that he would go against their agreement and spill the beans in such a way. He hadn't even been around Kyler long enough for him to be even remotely be able to explain things to him. No wonder her damn son had come home looking crazy. She didn't even know what to say to. For a second, she considered lying and saying that Zyree wasn't his father. It was obvious that's what he was waiting for. For some reason though she just couldn't.

Instead she let her anger take over and went to slip into her shoes that were by the door. She snatched Kyler's hand in hers and left on her way to curse Zyree the fuck out before she let *him* explain things. By now, Kyler had tears in his eyes because her silence had pretty much given him his answer.

The trek to Zyree's house was short, and Anastasia was happy to see that his car was there as she banged on his door. He didn't even ask who it was before swinging it open like he already knew who was there. Instead of airing their dirty laundry on his porch Anastasia brushed past him and stepped inside of his foyer with a scowl, but as soon as the door was closed and she'd directed Kyler into his living room she finally opened her mouth to speak.

"You got some muthafuckin nerve! How dare you just spring that shit on him like that with no explanation!" she ranted.

"I did explain! How long was I sposed to wait, huh? Leave it to you he wouldn't ever find out! He would have went his whole life thinkin I was the nigga from down the street," he said pointing to himself.

"You was sposed to wait until I said so, I don't give a fuck how long I made you wait!" It was crazy to her how he didn't understand what he'd done. Just because he was Kyler's real father that didn't give him the right to traumatize their son.

"Well, now we don't have to wait do we? He knows and we can be a family like we're sposed to-."

"We're not gonna be a family!" Anastasia screamed in frustration, garnering a strange look from Zyree. She was tired of going back and forth with him about the same thing. Maybe they shouldn't have even tried to do the whole letting Kyler get to know him thing. It was obvious to her that the nigga was crazy as hell and she didn't want him to do anything that could hurt her or her son. She was definitely telling D'Mani about this shit.

"Ok, I see how it is. I guess you need to be heading back home then, right?" he said in a somber voice.

"Look I'm not trying to keep you away from Kyler, I just need you to be patient with him, and let this whole family thing go. I'm with D'Mani and I'm staying with him." He nodded and mumbled an "ayite" before motioning that she could leave.

Against her better judgement she called out to Kyler and he came running around the corner, ready to get out of there just like she was.

"Ok, I'll message or call you about getting him again," she said, taking Kyler's hand and turning to leave. She didn't even get a chance to hear a response, if he even responded because the next thing she knew she felt a sharp pain in the back of her head and everything went dark.

Anastasia sat up and looked around confused. She was definitely not at home and she could barely remember anything after coming to talk to Zyree. The room was dark, but she could see that it was a regular bedroom with white furniture. She was on the bed, covered up like she was taking a nap, and when she went to move she realized that her hands were cuffed to the headboard. "What the fuck? Zyree! Zyree!" she yelled out realizing that the nigga had basically knocked her out and kidnapped her. She wondered where the hell her son was as she continued to scream until the door opened and bright light filled the room.

"Stop screaming before you wake up Kyler," Zyree hissed. He came closer to the bed, dressed in some basketball shorts and a wife beater like he'd been in bed himself.

"What the fuck you mean stop screamin, let me the fuck go and get my son! Where is he? You bet not have hurt him!" she said looking around frantically. She knew his ass was crazy, but not kidnap people crazy!

"No, I think you need some more time to consider us being a family, and what better way to do that than to stay here with me." He shrugged like what he was saying was normal." Ky's fine, it took him awhile, but he went to sleep, if you wake him up though I'm not gon' be happy. Shit, it took a long time to get his ass to lay down, I had to give him somethin."

Anastasia's face twisted in horror at him. What were the odds that the man who raised her son AND his father were both out of their god damn minds? Only in the Holiday family would some shit like this happen. She wanted to remain tough, but she was really scared. If the nigga was willing to knock her out in front of her son it wasn't no telling what else he would do.

"What the fuck you mean gave him something? You bet not have drugged my baby!"

"I ain't drug him, it was only Benadryl." he said. "Now relax, y'all both gone be here for a while." He moved closer and Anastasia fought against her restraints. She quickly realized that she wasn't going anywhere and could only turn her head away from him as he tried to kiss her on the lips. He let out a chuckle. "You always have been a lil bit feisty."

"Fuck you! I hope you know my nigga comin for me-."

"Oh, I'm hopin for it." He smiled like he was demented and backed out of the room. Anastasia suddenly wished that she had took the time to tell D'Mani where she was going, or stayed her ass home and waited for him, then her and Kyler wouldn't even be in this mess. Luckily, although she knew he was out of his rabbit mind, she didn't think that he would hurt them. All he kept talking about was his family so that was what he wanted. She figured if she pretended to want to be in his life the way he wanted them to then she had a better chance of getting away.

Just as she was about to call out to him the sound of a big "boom" shook the entire house. She could hear a rumble of voices barking downstairs and took that as her cue to start screaming wildly. It was maybe five minutes or less before the bedroom door opened again and what looked to be a SWAT team came inside with their guns drawn.

"Help me! He kidnapped me and my son! I don't know where he is!" she shrieked and they all looked at each other like they weren't sure they should believe her. A tall white man stepped into the room with his bald head glistening and demanded that they uncuff her.

"Anastasia, I'm detective Moore, we've been building a case against Zyree for almost a year, which is probably why he came here to New York. We've got your son already, he's a little disoriented but he seems fine otherwise." He informed her once they'd gotten the cuffs off and she was standing. That was all news to her because Zyree hadn't even been acting like a man on the run.

"That's because his crazy ass drugged my baby! Where is he?" she spat. As angry as she sounded, she was really extremely grateful that they'd come when they did. All she wanted was to be able to see her son and make sure for herself that he was okay.

"He's right this way, in addition to the drug charges he's already facing I'll make sure that he is also tried for this shit as well." He lead her out of the room and downstairs where they had Kyler sitting on the couch being looked at by a paramedic. Anastasia damn near pushed the lady out of the way to get to him and swooped him up into a hug. She held him against her and cried.

"I'm so sorry, baby," she told him as she rocked him like he was a damn baby. He didn't say anything but he held her neck back just as tightly.

After the paramedic gave her the ok on Kyler they asked if she needed to be checked out but she declined. All she wanted to do was return to the safety of her own home. The detective took her statement and then finally told her she was free to go. As she carried Kyler's heavy ass out of the house she looked around at the chaos that was going on outside. Zyree's yard was full of different police and FBI agents and the neighbors were all out on their lawns. She passed by everyone not wanting to talk to anyone else. When she got to the unmarked car that was directly in front of his house she didn't even notice that Zyree was in there until he tried to call out to her. She ignored his crazy ass and kept going. From what the detective had told her he wasn't going to be getting out for a long time and she was more than happy about that. Maybe now, her and her family could get the happily ever after they all deserved.

Chapter 26

Waking up with Corey's head between her thighs got Alyssa's day started on the right foot. She was kind of in a funk since Corey checked Johnathan at the cookout and quit her job for her. Alyssa spent her days searching for information on Felix and being as though she didn't have the resources she once had, it was difficult to find anything on her suspect. Alyssa tried to follow him during the day but Felix was all about business when the sun was up and if she was going to catch him doing anything shady, she needed to have eyes on his ass at night which was something she couldn't do. She didn't want or need Corey having any suspicions of her. Feeling defeated, she decided to chalk her mission of revenge up as a fail before calling Andrea and letting her know. Her older sister was determined to continue her search for dirt on Felix and Alyssa knew she would be successful.

Besides searching for information on Drea's ex friend, Alyssa spent her time searching for houses in Georgia. After being there for Lexi's graduation and since Drea was living there with the twins, she was strongly considering moving to Georgia. Alyssa searched for houses that were close to Atlanta and instantly fell in love with all of the homes she saw. Alyssa saved many of the homes she found in the neighboring cities of Atlanta. She wasn't sure how her husband would feel about the move. Corey had only been at his job for a few months and Alyssa wasn't sure if he would want to move at the moment but she was hoping for the best.

After satisfying her husband's sexual and hunger needs, Corey left for work in great spirits. After locking the front door, Alyssa scurried to the bathroom removing the pregnancy test she hid in the pocket of her bathrobe. She stared at the box for a moment reading the instructions. She took a deep breath before ripping the box open and taking the test. When she was finished,

Alyssa washed her hands and sat on the edge of the tub as she waited for the results. She couldn't believe that she went nearly two months without realizing that she was late on her period. Alyssa had a lot of ups and downs over the past few months and she truly didn't know if she was pregnant or if she missed her period due to stress. Alyssa purchased the pregnancy test just to ease her own mind. As much as she wanted the results to be positive, she didn't have high expectations. Getting up from the tub, Alyssa walked over to the sink to read the test. Seeing the results had her floored. The positive test that laid on the sink caused a smile to spread across her lips.

"Oh, my God. I'm really pregnant." Alyssa smiled as she held up the test.

Placing the test back on the sink, she walked into her bedroom snatching her phone off the nightstand and calling her mom. Victoria answered on the third ring.

"Hey Alyssa. How you doin', baby?"

"I'm doing fine, mama. How about you?"

"I can't complain. Just happy to be alive."

"How you doin', Heffa?" Aunt Shirley yelled in the background.

"Hi Aunt Shirley," she replied dryly rolling her eyes.

"I got you on speaker phone because I got a feelin' you're about to tell me somethin' good?"

"Yes ma'am. I'm pregnant, mom." Alyssa smiled.

"Oh, my goodness! I'm gonna have another grandbaby! This news just brightened my day!" her mother shouted. "Did you tell Corey yet?"

"Not yet. I'm gonna surprise him with the test when he gets home from work tonight," she beamed.

"You just couldn't let your sister be great, huh? Right after she have her babies, here you come talkin' bout you pregnant. The hate is real honey," Aunt Shirley added her two cents.

"Ain't nobody hating on Drea, okay? I can't help that I got pregnant at this time."

"And if you ask me, you sound like the hater, Shirley. Now, leave my child alone and stop ruining her moment. Damn!"

"Thanks mama."

Victoria put her on hold but she could hear Aunt Shirley talking to her man in the background. When Alyssa heard her aunt tell Ronald that the snitch is pregnant, she was ready to cuss her ass out but decided to leave it alone. Even with a man in her life, Aunt Shirley was still a pain in her ass. When her mother came back to the phone, they chopped it up for a few minutes before bringing their call to an end. Placing her phone back on the nightstand, Alyssa went back into the bathroom to get washed and dressed for the day. After doing her hair, she snatched up her purse and phone then headed out the door. When she was comfortably seated behind the wheel, Alyssa received a text from Elaine telling her to meet her in the parking lot of her job ASAP. Starting the engine, Alyssa pulled off down the block.

As she made her way to Elaine, Alyssa was having second thoughts about meeting her. Everything was on point with them and after learning that they were going to have an addition to their family, Alyssa didn't want anything to ruin her mood or her day with the information Elaine was about to present to her. Being as though she waited long enough to find out what her husband was up to, Alyssa decided to just go head and brace herself in case it was anything bad. Parking next to Elaine's car, she rolled her window down to greet her.

"Give it to me straight, E. Should I even look at this or can I just toss this and go about my day?" Alyssa got straight to the point.

"I wish I could tell you that you didn't have to open this but you definitely need to take a look inside this envelope," Elaine stated with a straight face.

Alyssa nodded her head at the heads up she just received before shaking Elaine's hand and thanking her for all the work she'd done for her. Watching her walk away and getting into her car, Alyssa took a deep breath before opening the white envelope and pulling out the pictures that were inside. The first picture she viewed was of Corey and a woman conversing in the lobby of a hotel. The next was a picture of him giving her money. When she came across a picture of Corey carrying a car seat out of the hotel, Alyssa almost lost it. There were pictures of him holding the baby but the expression on his face wasn't a joyful one. The next few pictures were of them going into a DNA clinic. The last photo was of him walking out the same clinic with an envelope in his hand. Alyssa assumed that it was the DNA results of the child he was with. Alyssa looked at the date on the last photo and saw that he went there that day. Tossing everything in the passenger seat, she pulled off and headed to the nearest party supply store.

Alyssa thought that shopping for her baby announcement materials would put her in a better mood but it didn't. How could she be happy about being pregnant when there was a possibility that her husband could possibly have a baby already? Alyssa had so many emotions running through her mind, but despite how she was feeling, she was going to remain calm and not let her thoughts get the best of her.

"Believe half of what you see and none of what you hear," she mumbled to herself.

After paying for the blue and pink balloons, gift box and gift bag, Alyssa left out of the store and headed back to her home. Before getting out her car, she stuffed the photos back in the envelope and stuffed the envelope under the passenger seat.

Alyssa didn't want Corey to know about the pictures. Once inside, she set up her pregnancy reveal surprise in her bedroom then got started on dinner. In the middle of her cooking dinner, her phone chimed indicating she had text. Checking her phone, Alyssa saw it was from Corey.

Corey: I got off work early. Be home in twenty minutes. We need to talk.

Alyssa: Okay. See you soon.

Alyssa finished up the food just as Corey was making his way inside the house. She took a deep breath before turning around to greet her husband but when she saw the yellow envelope in his hand, it caused her to freeze in place.

"Hey Bae," Corey greeted her.

"Hey." She forced a small smile. "What's that?"

"This is what I need to talk to you about, Alyssa." He held up the envelope.

They both took a seat at the counter and as much as she was ready to pounce on Corey, she decided to let him talk. He placed the envelope on the counter face down before he spoke.

"You remember around Christmas time, I showed you the text from the chick I cheated on with you sayin' that she was lyin' and what not?"

"Yeah."

"The day we came home from our honeymoon, she texted me tellin' me that her boyfriend wasn't the father of her baby. So, she assumed I was." Corey paused.

Alyssa bit the inside of her cheek.

"Is that the reason why you didn't want kids?"

"Yes," he sighed.

She nodded her head at the answer but when Alyssa remained quiet, Corey continued.

"I ignored her at first but when she began makin' threats of tellin' you, I decided to comply with her demands which was money and to spend time with them. A month ago, I told her I wanted to take a paternity test. At first, she denied me but once I threatened to cut her off, she cooperated. Long story short, I haven't heard from her since I got tested but I have the results." Corey slid the envelope over to her.

"I haven't opened it yet because I wanted to wait until I got home. I want you to open the envelope though."

Staring at him for a few seconds, Alyssa grabbed it but Corey placed his hand over hers.

"You gotta promise me that no matter what the results say, you'll keep ya cool, you won't throw no punches and you won't leave me."

Alyssa stared into her husband's eyes and saw that he was afraid of losing her and what the results could be. She had no plans of leaving Corey but if the results were positive, Alyssa definitely wanted to lay hands on him but being as though her husband was having a rough time dealing with this, she decided to agree to his terms.

"I promise."

Releasing her hand, Alyssa opened the yellow envelope removing the paper. Carefully reading the results, she was relieved when she read that Corey was not the father of that child. Instead of expressing her happiness, she stared at the paper a few moments longer to make Corey nervous.

"What does it say?" Corey asked anxiously.

"Read this shit for yourself." Alyssa tossed the paper at him angrily.

Instantly dropping his head, Corey got up from the counter and began pacing the floor.

"I said read the results, Corey!"

Snatching the paper off the counter, she watched as Corey's demeanor changed.

"Yo, you play to fuckin' much, Lyssa." Corey shook his head.

Alyssa burst into laughter while Corey balled the paper up and threw it at her missing her by an inch.

"That's why you missed punk." She continued to laugh.

Alyssa got up from the counter before Corey could make it to her. Running to the bedroom, she left the door open so he could see the gift bag sitting on the bed with the pink and blue balloons tied to it. When Corey saw the bag, he stopped dead in his tracks.

"What's this?"

"Look inside and see." Alyssa smirked.

Alyssa twiddled her thumbs as she watched her husband removed the lid from the watch box she put the pregnancy test in. His eyes grew wide and Alyssa couldn't help but laugh.

"Is this for real? You're.... you really pregnant right now?"

"Yeah bae. I took the test this morning after you left." Alyssa smiled.

The smile that spread across his lips warmed Alyssa's heart as Corey made his way over to her hugging her tightly in his arm. Alyssa was beyond happy that her husband shared her joy about her being pregnant. Even though she was rattled about Corey fathering another woman's child, Alyssa was glad that she remained calmed and didn't go off on him like she wanted to. With her day being a whirlwind of emotions, Alyssa was relieved it ended on a high note. Although she would've been devastated if the results were positive, she still would have stayed by her husband's side. They were in this for better or for worse and no matter what, they were staying together through it all.

Chapter 27

Lexi grabbed a family size bag of Cheddar Ruffles potato chips and placed them in the shopping cart. After doing so, she then made her way one aisle over, where she grabbed a twenty-four pack of Dasani water. Just as she began to lift it, she heard Aunt Shirley's voice echoing through her ears as if she was on a PA system.

"You bet not lift that heavy shit. Didn't you just get out the hospital," she barked.

"Auntie, I'm good and besides, it's not that heavy."

"You better leave it right there. Marcus, take yo Flamin Hot eating ass over there and pick up that water," she demanded.

Marcus cut his eyes at Shirley before following her orders.

"I don't care how much twist you put in yo walk, you a man at the end of the day," she lectured.

"I don't see how y'all deal with her ass," Marcus whispered to Lexi just as Andrea turned the corner with hot dog buns.

"I hear y'all fussing from the other side of the store, what's going on?" she questioned.

"Nothing except that Lexi trying to lift shit like she just wasn't involved in a car accident that resulted in her having a miscarriage a few weeks ago." Aunt Shirley filled her in.

"Alexis, now you know better," Andrea scolded.

"I'm good y'all. Chill," she advised them before taking out her phone and checking the grocery list she had saved in her notes.

It had been almost a month since the car accident and miscarriage and Lexi was starting to feel like herself again. Although she never wanted to keep the baby, seeing how much losing the baby hurt J.R., had an effect on her. They hadn't talked much about it since it happened. Working hard and staying busy was the way he was coping with the pain and as for Lexi, she spent as much time with her sister, niece and nephew as she could. She even started remodeling the club, which was something she enjoyed doing.

"Aye Lexi look, ain't that…." Marcus stated, causing Lexi to look up from her phone.

"Tamika Loving My Man Wells," the two of them said in unison as they stared at the woman who inboxed Lexi a month ago about J.R.

"Yeah that's that bitch," Lexi confirmed as she placed the Oreo cookies that was in her hand inside the cart.

She slowly walked over to the female with Marcus in tow.

"Who the fuck is that?" Aunt Shirley quizzed.

"Chile, I think that's the woman who claimed she was fucking with J.R.," Andrea filled her in as they both looked along.

"Your sister about to beat that girl ass in this Walmart and I ain't gon stop her," Shirley said, wrapping her salt and pepper hair up in a bun before joining Lexi and Marcus.

"So, bitch, you wanna send old ass pictures and shit?" Alexis walked right up to her and asked.

"Huh?" Tamika replied, clearly caught off guard.

"Shorty, don't act like you don't know what it is. I should beat yo ass just off the strength of you lying," Lexi informed her.

"Look all that won't even be necessary., Tamika's friend chimed in.

"Girl, you can get these hands first," Marcus turned to her and stated, forcing her to take a few steps back.

"Look, I don't know you and you don't know me," Tamika replied.

"But you knew me enough to inbox me with some bullshit. I could drag you through this store but I see you scared and one thing I'm not, is a bully but be clear, if you ever see me again, I suggest you turn the other way and leave because this hall pass in only good for today," Lexi explained.

Without any further words being exchanged, Tamika and her friend left their cart right where it was and exited the store.

"Awww Baby Holiday, I'm so proud of you," Andrea gushed as she hugged her little sister.

"Bitch, get off of me." Lexi laughed, yanking away from their embrace.

The four of them, got the last items they needed for the Fourth of July barbeque and headed back to Drea's house. As soon as they pulled up, the smell of ribs, hot links and steak crept into their nostrils. Alexis's stomach began to growl, she couldn't wait to eat. Her mother had made her a special bowl of her infamous tuna fish and she couldn't wait to attack it.

"Marcus ,get that damn water!" Aunt Shirley yelled out to him before heading into the house.

Marcus smacked his lips but lifted the waters out of the trunk and brought them in. Alexis still couldn't believe how beautiful Drea's house was. She also still couldn't believe that her sister lived so close to her. Which made her reconsider moving to New York for graduate school. Yeah, she'd have Stasia and Lyssa close by but she'd feel incomplete without Drea, Aunt Shirley and her mom being even further away. Not to mention, J.R. and her new club, moving to New York seemed impossible.

"Looks like someone is woke," Victoria said, wiping her hands on her apron as the twins cried out from their room.

"I'll get them mom," Drea said, rushing off to her babies while everyone else put the food up.

Andrea returned to the kitchen with a fussing AJ in hand. She tried rocking her, feeding her but nothing seemed to work.

"What's the matter Princess, you want your daddy?" D'Mari appeared from the backyard, taking AJ from Drea.

Mari rocked and tried feeding her as well but to no avail.

"Give me my granddaughter, her might be gassy?" Their mother said before washing her hands and taking AJ.

Victoria tried different ways of soothing before Lexi stepped in.

"Awww TT Baby, they don't know what they doing," Lexi cooed.

As soon as AJ snuggled up inside of Lexi's arms, she stopped crying.

"Ain't that a bitch," Drea cursed, causing everyone to laugh.

"Y'all don't know how to handle Alexis Jr.," Lexi said, sticking out her tongue as she took a seat at the kitchen table.

"Look bruh, I think it's time y'all try again at this parenting thing cuz Lexi looking like a pro." D'Mari said to J.R. who joined them in the house.

Mari had no idea how much tension his comment caused amongst the young couple. Parenting was a subject that they tried to avoid the best way possible. Lexi looked up in time to catch J.R. staring at her. She gave him a warm smile, before tending back to AJ who had fallen asleep.

"I'm about to go lay her down, I'll be back," she said, standing to her feet and heading upstairs.

Once in their room, she laid her niece down, gave her a few pats on the back before turning to leave.

"Shit, you scared me." She jumped at the sight of J.R. who was standing behind her.

Instead of replying, he grabbed her by the waist and pulled her close.

"I love you, shorty!" he said, licking his lips.

"I love you, too, shorty!" She blushed, standing on her tippy toes, planting a kiss on his lips.

"I know you not ready for any kids but…."

Lexi silenced him by placing her index finger to his lips. She then grabbed him by the hand, leading him out the room and down the hall to the bathroom. Once inside, she closed the door and began kissing him. She wasn't sure what had come over her but she missed her man and although he was physically around, their connection had been off since the miscarriage.

"Lexi, what you doing, yo whole family downstairs," he said, as she tugged on his Gucci belt.

"Since when you ever gave a fuck?" She paused and asked him.

"You right," was all he said before lifting her up on the sink.

The cream sundress she wore made for easy access as J.R. pulled her panties to the side, dipping in her wetness.

"Bae, the doctor said six weeks." He stopped in mid-stroke and informed her.

"Fuck them doctors." Lexi bit her bottom lip before pushing him deeper inside her.

Both Lexi and J.R. tried to contain themselves with everyone being only a few feet away but it was a challenge for the both of them. Lexi felt J.R. inside her stomach, it was painful yet pleasuring and she didn't want him to stop but they both knew this was a quickie so they had to hurry before they got caught.

"Fuck baby, I'm finna come," he moaned, just before he emptied his load inside of her.

Lexi wrapped her legs around him tighter as she rode the wave. After they were done, they grabbed two hand towels from Drea's closet and cleaned themselves up before heading back downstairs. When they arrived, the house was empty but Aunt Shirley's big mouth could be heard from the backyard. Making their way to them, they walked through the kitchen, slid the doors back and as expected, all eyes were on them.

"It take that long to lay a baby down?" Drea quizzed.

"Nah, but it take that long to make one. Up top fav.," Aunt Shirley said before slapping fives with Lexi.

"Alexis, you bet not, you know what the doctors said," their mother scolded.

"I know, Ma. I know."

Lexi held her head low because regardless of how grown she was, talking about sex with her mother still didn't sit right with her.

"So, what's going on with Graduate School?" Victoria asked, changing the subject, which made Lexi happy.

"Well, I didn't know if I wanted to tell y'all or not but, I got accepted into a school in New York," she said, finally spilling the beans.

"Oh, my God, that's great baby!" her mother beamed.

"But why you didn't want to tell us?" Andrea asked.

"Because, I'm having second thoughts. With you living here now and my club and my man..." she said, glancing at J.R. "I really don't want to," she continued.

"Well sister, you do know that there are more schools than just that one in New York," Drea advised her.

"Yeah, I know, which is why I sort of eighty-sixth that idea."

"But ma, have you thought about moving here?" Lexi asked.

"Chile, I'm too old to pick up and move," Victoria stated.

"Too old, ain't no such thing, Ma," J.R. added in.

"Exactly and besides, you need some new scenery," Drea chimed in.

"With you here, you can help Drea with the twins once she goes back to work. Me and you can be together every day.

Pleassseee Ma," Lexi begged, walking over to her and sitting on her lap.

"Well, if that'll make my baby girl happy then!"

"Oh my God, are you serious, Ma?" Lexi screamed, wrapping her arms around her mother's neck and squeezing it tight.

"So, just fuck me, huh? Ain't nobody gon beg me to move?" Aunt Shirley hissed.

"Fav, now you know. You just got a man though, you ready to leave him already?" Lexi turned to Shirley and asked.

"Chile, with this Grade A pussy I got, he'll be a Georgia Peach before you know it." She smiled.

Everyone laughed at Aunt Shirley who had absolutely no filter but you couldn't help but love her. Lexi was starting to feel good about the direction her life was heading in. Her mom was moving soon, her man was everything and more, her sister and family was only minutes away. Now, all she had to do was convince Alyssa and Anastasia to move definitely and her life in Atlanta would be complete.

Chapter 28

"Ahhh… shit Mari. Wait wait wait…"

"Nah, ain't no waiting. You talked all that shit last night and fell asleep before I could get some. You better take… this… dick…" he said in between thrusts.

It was true, the night before Drea had talked so much shit to D'Mari. He agreed to give both babies their baths and feed them and put them to bed. By the time he was done, Drea had showered and was knocked the fuck out. If Mari tried to wake her up, she didn't hear or feel a thing, but he woke her ass up bright and early with his tongue, followed by his thick, hard dick. He lifted her left leg over his shoulder and went deeper.

"Oh, my gawwddd… baby!! I'm bout to cum." Drea dug her nails into his back.

"Let that shit go," he grunted.

Just hearing those words, along with the pressure Mari was putting on her made Drea squirt all over the place. Not long after, Mari was releasing inside of her.

"Boy, why you didn't pull out," Drea fussed.

"Pussy too good to pull out. You know that," he said and kissed her.

"Nigga, I ain't tryna have no more kids. We got our boy and girl so we good." She playfully hit him.

"Well, if it happens, it happens. Now, get up so we can get our day started," he told her and headed for the bathroom.

Drea's alarm on her phone sounded as soon as she got up. She turned it off and looked at the date. It was July 10th, the day that she was initially given as a due date. D'Mari woke her up better than any alarm ever could and she smiled. He told her that he had a surprise for her, and she actually had a surprise for him as well. She had been thinking about it ever since the barbecue they had on the 4th of July. Her mom and Aunt Shirley had left the day before and Drea was missing them already, even her crazy ass aunt, but she had a feeling that they would be back soon. It was still strange being away from them but having D'Mari by her side day and night made everything better.

Before Drea could walk into her closet to pull something out to wear, she heard Ava crying through the monitor. Her little cries started out cute, but they could wreck your nerves if you didn't tend to her quickly, so Drea made her way to the nursery. The nanny that they hired had been there about five times getting familiar with them and she would be there within the next hour before Drea and D'Mari headed out. They thought it would be good to allow her to watch the babies for the day and even though Drea was nervous, she was excited at the same time in hopes that the day would be great.

When she made it to the room, Ava was still crying, but DJ was still knocked out. She changed Ava's diaper while talking to her, but it wasn't until she called the child AJ that she giggled.

"Damn, Lexi got my baby not answering to her real damn name," Drea fussed and made a mental note to cuss Lexi out again, not that it would be even matter.

After Ava had on a fresh diaper, Drea picked her up and then sat in the rocker and fixed her a bottle. She had gotten the multitasking down to a tee, but she prayed that DJ would stay asleep until she was done with Ava. Fifteen minutes and two big burps later, Ava was back sleeping peacefully. It was a blessing that the babies actually slept like newborns. They would stay awake if you held them, but for the most part if they weren't eating or being changed, they were sleeping. Before she could walk out of the room, DJ began to stir and Drea turned around and headed to his crib.

"I got lil man... go on and get dressed," Mari walked in and said and Drea didn't put up a fuss after thanking D'Mari.

A little over an hour later, Drea was giving the nanny last minute instructions as Mari rushed her out of the door. She knew that her babies were in good hands, she had prayed about it and Mrs. Sarah had been highly recommended in the area. They made their way to the truck and got in. Drea was dressed in a white flowy maxi dress that she had ordered from New York and Company in the Gabrielle Union Collection. At first, she didn't think that her curves would allow it to fit right, but she was pleasantly surprised. She topped the outfit off with some gold sandals and accessories.

"You look good as fuck, Ma," Mari said as he backed out of the driveway.

"You don't look too bad yourself." Drea smirked as she admired him dressed down in a white polo shirt and Khakis.

"So, where we going?" Drea quizzed after a few minutes of riding.

"You'll see in due time babe… chill out." Mari reached over and squeezed her leg.

Drea's phone rang and she saw that it was her mom calling so she cheerfully answered.

"Hey ma… how are you?"

"I'm just fine. How are you and my babies… and how is that man of yours? I shol hate that you aren't near, but I understand and I want you to be happy," Victoria rambled on and on not giving Drea a chance to answer.

"We're fine mom. Mari and I are headed out and the babies are with Mrs. Sarah."

"Okay… I like her. I'm glad I met her. I'm just so happy. All my girls are doing well. I hope Lyssa and Corey have a girl so Ava won't be the only girl."

"Lyssa's pregnant?" Drea cut Victoria off.

"Yeah baby… she didn't tell y'all yet. Well she probably waiting until she see y'all knowing her, but I'm happy."

"That's exciting… but I'm bout to light our group chat up."

Drea talked to her mom for a few more minutes and as soon as she hung up, she kept her word and went straight to the HS4 chat that Lexi had renamed.

Drea: Ummm Lyssa… do you have something to tell your sisters?

Lexi: Ooooh Drea I meant to call you last night after I hung up with Aunt Shirley. She said Lyssa got pregnant to steal your shine.

Stasia: Lyssa you pregnant?

Drea: She taking forever to reply but mama just told me. And Lexi how you forget to call me with info like that? Smh.

Lyssa: Sisters! I wanted to tell y'all in person when we get together on Labor Day. I meant to tell mom to keep it a secret, but I forgot. I'm sorry!

Drea: Hmph… I guess we forgive you.

Lexi: Drea, you don't speak for us. TF… but yeah, I guess we forgive you, Lyssa.

Stasia: I'll call you in a few, Lyssa. I'm a little mad, but I forgive you.

Drea: Okay y'all... me and Mari pulling up downtown. I got something to tell y'all later.

Drea put her phone up and filled D'Mari in on the news about Lyssa and Corey expecting. He said that Corey had called him a couple of days ago, but he forgot to hit him back. They parked and Drea was still a little clueless as to why they were downtown, but it was perfect for what she had in mind for later. They got out and Drea watched as Mari took a key from his pocket and opened a door to a building that looked brand new.

"Umm Mari... what is this?" she quizzed, but he only smirked and walked inside.

She followed him and walked into one of the most beautiful office spaces that she had ever laid eyes on. There was brand new furniture, but it was clear that no one had ever worked there.

"I know you thought you would have a headache finding your own office space and furnishing it, but this is it. Everything is good to go and your new law firm can open whenever you're ready to return to work."

"D'Mari Mitchell... you did not. This is mine? I mean, this is OURS?"

"It's yours, baby. Now, all I need you to do is tell me the name of it so I can order the signs."

Drea stood there in awe as tears rolled down her cheeks. It felt like her life had become a movie and she didn't want it to end.

"Thank you so much, baby... that one-night stand changed my life and I swear I would do it all over again if I had to choose. I love you so much."

"I love you, too, baby. And I told you I got you. Stop thanking me for doin shit I'm supposed to do." He walked over and pulled her in for a hug.

"HS4 & Associates... I wanna continue branding the name Lexi came up with. She's gonna be the accountant here. I might even have to hire Lyssa since she can't keep a job. Oh, my God I'm so excited," Drea rambled on.

"Perfect... I'll have all the signs installed by next week. Now, let's view the rest of the building and then go get something to eat."

After they finished looking around, Drea was pleased. D'Mari had thought of everything. When they walked back out the door, Drea grabbed D'Mari's hand and pulled him in the opposite direction than where they parked.

Where we goin?" he asked.

"Don't ask questions, just come with me."

They made their way to the courthouse, and Drea saw how Mari tensed up.

"Relax baby." She laughed.

They made their way inside and Drea asked for Judge Simpson. The receptionist picked up the phone and made a call. When she hung up, Drea was told where to go. They took the elevator up to the third floor and walked to the third door on the right.

"Andrea Holiday... are y'all ready to do this?" Judge Simpson asked while smiling.

"You ready to be my husband?" Drea turned to Mari.

"You serious? You don't want a wedding? What about your family?" Mari asked question after question after question.

"All I need is you. You've done everything in your power to make me happy and I don't wanna go another day without being Mrs. Andrea Mitchell. And what better day to do than that would have been my due date if we woulda made it?" she sincerely replied.

"Well let's do this then." Mari kissed her.

"We'll get to that part in a minute." The judge laughed and interrupted them.

Drea pulled all of the paperwork as well as Mari's ring from her purse and they got started. Shortly afterwards, she kissed her man and felt complete. Drea took a picture of their marriage license and sent it to her sisters. She knew that a group FaceTime call was about to come through and before they left out the door, Lexi was calling and cussing her out. After she hung up with her Baby Holiday, her phone rang again and Drea just knew that it was one of her other sister, but when she saw Felix name pop on the screen, she froze a little.

"What's wrong?" Mari asked.

"I finally get to handle this shit," Drea said and answered the call.

"Felix Alexander," she answered and she saw Mari's jaw clench at the name.

Drea knew that her man wanted to handle the shit, but she had a better way.

"Andrea Holiday…"

"It's Andrea Mitchell now, but I'm glad you called so I can get this shit outta the way. After doing a little research I found out about that fee that was paid to the board on your behalf. I would advise you to leave me the fuck alone unless you want that valuable piece of information to get out," Drea calmy stated.

The silence on the line let her know that her point was made. She hung up without giving him any extra time to respond.

"You good, babe? You know I'll take care of that shit," Mari told her.

"It's all good, baby… everything is all good." Drea smiled and kissed her husband.

Chapter 29

After missing the Fourth of July with her family, Alyssa was sad and ready to throw her whole condo away and move to Georgia. Every time that Lexi and Drea FaceTimed her aand Stasia, it made Lyssa sad, but she kept her composure. Besides wanting to be closer to her sisters, she was ready for her and Corey to become homeowners and begin a new chapter in their lives. After she revealed to Corey that she was pregnant, Alyssa told him that she was wanted to move to Georgia. Being as though Corey was New York to the core, she thought that she would really have to sell him on the idea of moving to another state but to Alyssa's surprise, she didn't. Corey was excited about moving and was fully onboard. Not wasting any time, they began their house search immediately.

Two weeks had passed when Corey called her from work and told her to start packing which was like music to Alyssa's ears. Instead of asking questions, she started packing their things. When he arrived home later that night, Corey explained that his boss needed someone to fill in on a sports show in Atlanta for a week and if things went well, he would get the spot permanently. Alyssa was more than excited about Corey's new job possibility. They had plans to spend the upcoming weekend down there to go house shopping but since they had the opportunity to stay down there for a week, that was even better. Alyssa shot a message to her sisters in the group chat letting them know that she would be there by Sunday and they were hype. She learned that Drea was about to open her law firm and when her older sister offered her a job, Alyssa was shocked. Her sisters joked about how she couldn't keep a job before Alyssa told her sister she would think about coming to work for her. Even though she should've jumped at the chance to work at Drea's firm, Alyssa had gotten comfortable with being a stay at home wife, even if it was boring as hell.

After only a few days on the job, Corey informed her that the producer of the show offered him a full-time position on the midday sports show. Alyssa was more than happy for her husband and even more happy that they wouldn't be returning to New York. Worried about what they were going to do with things back home, Corey assured her that he would take care of everything while they continued to search for their new home.

Most of the houses they saw were beautiful but they were small on the inside. When they came across the tenth house on their list, Alyssa was sure that they had found their dream house but when the realtor informed them about the price increase for all the new installations and repairs, she became upset because Corey said it was out of their price range. Alyssa told him that they could get a loan from the bank but her husband was determined to pay for the home with his own money. She even offered to clean out her bank account to help pay for the house but Corey shot her down. Alyssa was pissed with his stubborn attitude but she was determined to get that house.

They had been staying at a hotel for the past month and when Corey denied her offer to help pay for the house a couple of weeks ago, Alyssa decided to accept her sister's job offer. If Corey didn't want to take her money or get a loan from the bank, she was ready do whatever it took to get the six-bedroom, five-bathroom house with the finished basement, newly renovated kitchen and back deck or something similar to it all by her damn self. Alyssa called her sister telling her she wanted to work for her and Andrea told her to come in at 10:00 am the next morning which was August 29th, a Monday and Alyssa was looking forward to it.

Waking up bright and early the next morning, Alyssa was feeling good about the interview she had with her sister but her body felt a little weird. When she was finished in the shower, Alyssa went over to the sink to brush her teeth a few seconds later, she suddenly became nauseous and rushed over to the toilet to vomit which caused Corey to come into the bathroom. When she finally stopped puking, Corey helped Alyssa to her feet after she flushed the toilet.

"You aight, Bae?"

"Yeah. I'm fine." She walked cover to the sink to rinse her mouth out.

"I had just started brushing my teeth when I felt the sudden urge to throw up. I guess the baby doesn't like tooth paste," she chuckled.

"Damn. The baby won't even let you brush ya grill? That's crazy."

"Yeah. I know." Alyssa shook her head.

"Baby, are you sure you wanna go back to work? I told you that I got you. I don't mind you not workin'." Corey pulled her close to him.

"I understand that, bae. But, I want that house and since you won't let me help you get it, I'm gonna go back to work, stack my bread and get the house myself," she seriously replied.

"And I'm tired of being cooped up in this hotel. I can be sitting on my ass at work making money instead of being here and being broke."

"I guess I can't change ya mind?"

"No."

"Aight. Let me get ready so I can drive you over there."

Corey walked out the bathroom leaving Alyssa alone. She reapplied the toothpaste to the brush and stared at it for a minute.

"Aight little one. Mommy needs to brush her teeth. So, don't get queasy and make me throw up again."

Successfully brushing her teeth, Alyssa went into the bedroom and got ready for the day. The pencil skirt she wanted to wear was too tight around her stomach. So, she decided on a maxi skirt, tank top and sandals. After making sure she had everything, the couple left the room and headed out the hotel. They arrived at Drea's office building thirty minutes early which was good because Alyssa wanted to impress her sister and show her that she was serious about working for her company. Alyssa pecked Corey's lips before getting out of the car and heading inside. She was about to call out for Drea until Alexis came out from behind one of the cubicles.

"Wassup hoe?" Lexi smiled.

"Hey Lexi," she greeted her sister.

"I see you're here early for ya interview."

"Yup and I'm ready to get started. So, where is Drea?"

"She stepped out for a minute. So, come on so we can get started." Lexi began to walk away.

"Wait a minute! Andrea agreed to let you do my damn interview?" Alyssa pointed at Lexi in disbelief.

"That's right, hoe, and you better watch ya mouth because your interview started when I told ya ass to follow me. Now, let's go." Lexi smirked as she walked off.

Words couldn't express how pissed off Alyssa was. She felt like Andrea told Alexis to do her interview to be smart. Alyssa was about say to hell with this job and walk out the door but decided not to. Instead, she took a deep breath and told herself to act professional. Even if her baby sister acted the complete opposite. As soon as she dropped her ass in the seat, Lexi requested her resume. Alyssa watched her as she looked over her resume that was attached to her clipboard. She knew by the way Alexis cut her eyes at her that she was about to say some slick shit to her. Her sister inquired about her short stay at the PI firm and the FBI like she didn't already know the reason behind that shit. After Alyssa explained the reason for her short time at her last couple of jobs, Lexi had the nerve to tell her that she felt like Alyssa was unreliable, unstable and inadequate in the jobs she was working. She was ready to kick her baby sister's ass behind the comment she made but she managed to keep her composure.

After thirty minutes of Alexis firing shots at her, her sister reluctantly gave her the position as the Legal Secretary/Assistant. Alyssa sarcastically thanked her before she got up to leave. As she headed to the door, Andrea walked in with a big smile on her face which confirmed that she knew what she was doing by telling Lexi to interview her. Alyssa gave Andrea a piece of her mind before the three of them laughed the situation off and hugged it out. The sisters chopped it up for a little bit and she neglected to tell them about how she puked that morning trying to brush her teeth. Wrapping up their conversation, Andrea told her that she could start tomorrow before Alyssa walked out the door.

Expecting her husband to still be parked in the same spot, Alyssa was annoyed when she saw that Corey was gone. She pulled out her phone but before she could call, he pulled up honking his horn.

"Hey baby. How was the interview?"

"Alexis was my interviewer. Need I say more?" She chuckled.

"Andrea is dead wrong for that. I know she gave ya ass a hard time." Corey laughed as he pulled off.

"You know she did. Needless to say, I got the job." She shook her head. "But enough of that. Where are you coming from?"

"I had to meet the realtor to pick up the keys to our new house," he spoke calmly.

"New house?" What new house?" She scooted to the edge of the seat.

"The house we looked at a few weeks back. You know, that one you loved and I didn't want to take out the loan for." Corey smirked.

"Stop playing with me, Corey."

Alyssa watched him as he removed the paperwork from his back pocket along with a set of keys. Reading over the paperwork, her smile grew wider and wider. Corey really purchased the house Alyssa was going so hard for. She threw her arms around her husband's neck and smothered his face with kisses as she repeatedly thanked him. Even though she had the proof right there in her hand that they were homeowners, Alyssa was still in disbelief. She couldn't believe that Corey bought the house after he told her they couldn't afford it. She was overwhelmed by the good news he presented her with and couldn't wait until they got back to their room to properly thank him after he fed her and their growing bundle of joy.

Chapter 30

After the whole ordeal with Zyree kidnapping her and Kyler, Anastasia was long overdue to be around family. Arriving in Atlanta the first thing she wanted to do was stop by Drea's new house to see the babies. Without even taking any of their bags to the hotel they drove straight there and she wasn't surprised at all to see Lexi was already there.

"   Hey, sisters!" she shrieked after Drea let her in. Kyler came in behind her with D'Mani in tow.

"Hey sister!"

"Hey bitch, I'm glad you made it, but don't think you bouta come win favorite TeTe either," Lexi quipped looking like she was ready to take off and get the twins before she could see them.

"Girl, you ain't favorite nothin, you just the one they been seeing the most," Anastasia said and rolled her eyes. She already knew that Lexi was going to be extra stingy with the twins or at least try to be, but she wasn't going to let her hold them hostage while she was there.

"Whatever, hey nephew, hey bro." Lexi waved her off and greeted the guys. Of course, Kyler was happy to see his Aunties and ran over to hug them while D'Mani gave her a chilled wave. He was still a little upset about Zyree getting off easy in his opinion. Anastasia had to talk him out of having somebody kill his ass in jail. Though he deserved many things, Anastasia didn't think he needed to die. He was already spending his life in prison pretty much, so they didn't need to be worried about him at all.

"Y'all need to quit, they're gonna love all y'all the same," Drea chided. She seemed to be so happy lately and Anastasia was glad that her sister was enjoying life.

"Ain't no equal nothin, this shis gone be split ten, ten, eighty," Lexi fussed. "Ava probably ain't even gone let them hold her."

"I bet she do, where they at Drea?" Stasia questioned and looked around the living room. The twins were across the room laying quietly in two bassinets.

"I'm bouta go see D right quick," D'Mani grumbled. "Come on Ky," he said and Kyler hurried to follow behind him.

Anastasia cringed a little at him calling Kyler, Ky. Ever since crazy ass Zyree had started calling him that it rubbed her the wrong way a little bit. She would never tell D'Mani that though, and Kyler didn't seem fazed at all anyway. After everything had went down Anastasia explained to Kyler that Richard was his father and Zyree was just sick in the head. It was the only way to avoid him growing up traumatized, knowing all of the stuff that had happened to his family. Anastasia made it across the room and swooped up a sleeping Ava first and began rocking her. She was a gorgeous little bundle of pink with thick curls of hair.

"Awwww." Anastasia cooed. She had always wanted a girl to dress up and talk to. When the baby didn't cry she gave Lexi a look and stuck out her tongue. "See, she likes me already."

"She sleep bitch, she don't know who titties she on right now." By now her and Drea were sitting on the couch next to where she stood, and Drea rolled her eyes at her sisters.

"Y'all cut that shit out," she warned jokingly before she took in Stasia. "What's wrong with D'Mani though, he seems grumpy?"

"Yeah, he was dry as hell speaking," Lexi added. Realizing that she had yet to tell her sisters about what happened. Anastasia laid baby Ava down and picked up DJ, before taking a seat herself. She quickly filled her sisters in on what had happened with Zyree and both of their faces wore full of shock.

"Damn, are y'all okay? How's Kyler taking this?" Drea asked.

"I'm more than okay, especially knowing we don't have to see his crazy ass no more. Kyler, he seems fine, but you just never know. He's already so quiet."

"Well, you should take him to go see somebody. Everything he's been through, it's no telling what type of psychological damage he can have."

"Hell yeah! He probably gone be fucked up if you don't. He done got snatched up by his fake daddy and his real daddy! I knew you shouldn't have done that shit," Lexi said shaking her head. Anastasia looked at her crazy because her and Aunt Shirley had been the main ones pressing the issue.

"Now you know-." She started but was interrupted by the doorbell chiming.

"Whoop! Let me go get that." Lexi hopped up and hurried away to answer the door before Anastasia could finish.

"You know that girl crazy." Drea chuckled. "But for real, have Kyler talk to somebody. I'm worried about him."

"I'll make sure I do that. I don't need more problems considering that D'Mani already is upset since he wanted to handle Zyree himself."

"Well, that I can't give you advice on. You know those twins of ours, once they have their minds made up." Anastasia couldn't argue with her about that. D'Mani and D'Mari were definitely stubborn when it came to things they wanted.

"Hey girls!" They looked up to see their mother entering the room and immediately went to hug her.

"Hey mama. I thought you wasn't comin till tomorrow?" Drea asked smiling.

"Well I was, but I just couldn't stay away another day! I'm trying to see my grandbabies," she exclaimed causing the sisters to laugh. Anastasia knew the whole time they were all there it was going to be a struggle over the twins. She handed DjJ over to her reluctantly and watched as she smothered him with kisses and baby talk.

"Where Lexi go?" Drea asked looking behind her mother.

"Her and Shirley out there smokin them weeds." She waved with a frown, causing Drea and Stasia to laugh. Their mother had never been a big fan of the way those two indulged.

They all went back into the living room as their mother raved about Drea's house. Anastasia agreed that D'Mari had done an excellent job, it was beautiful and she couldn't wait to see the rest of it.

"This house big as hell!" They heard their Aunt shout from the foyer, just before her and Lexi walked into the room with low eyes.

"I told you, Aunty," Lexi said coming further into the room and plopping down on the couch. Aunt Shirley stood in place and spun around nodding in approval.

"This is one nice ass house! I knew it was a reason I like them boys. They all fine as hell and paid." Anastasia shook her head at Shirley knowing she was going to be doing a lot of that with her crazy Aunt around.

"Aunt Shirley, you got a man though," she said with pursed lips.

"Well, it don't hurt to upgrade, Stasia. Shit, I was gone stay with my favorite so I could steal that fine ass man she got, but I think I'm gone stay here now."

"You wasn't staying at my crib noway," Lexi spoke and pulled a bag of candy out of her pocket.

"All y'all so stingy damn! It's enough of them niggas to go around!" Shirley fussed.

"Shirley, you got a man, leave these girls alone," their mother finally said.

"Girls?? These heffas all grown, Victoria! They ain't been girls in a long time."

"Well, they're still my girls, so leave 'em alone."

Shirley grumbled under her breathe and went to sit down next to Lexie. Their Aunt was too much sometimes. After they all finished laughing, they just talked about everything that had been going on while they waited for Alyssa who ended up coming thirty minutes later, with Corey in tow. It was a nice first day even though they didn't wind up doing anything but enjoying each other's company.

Later that night after she had gotten Kyler to bed Stasia sat contemplating whether or not she was going to accept the job that Lexi had offered her. As far as she knew Alyssa had already done so and she wondered if she should, too. There was really nothing for them in New York, and her family was all moving to Atlanta. She didn't see any reason why she shouldn't make that move too.

"So, are you done being mad?" Anastasia asked D'Mani when he entered the room after his shower. Her eyes roamed his naked body from head to foot and she couldn't help but feel blessed.

"Never said I was mad," he told her with his back turned. She watched the way it flexed as he threw on a tank top and some boxers before sliding into bed beside her.

"Well, what is wrong then? Cause you been actin funny ever since that night at Zyree's." She turned on her side so that they could talk. D'Mani let out a sigh like he didn't want to have this conversation.

"I just don't like that I wasn't there when y'all needed me. What if that crazy ass nigga had hurt y'all or somethin?"

"Well, he didn't thankfully, but you're always there for me and Kyler. You've been more of a father to him in such a short amount of time than Richard had his whole life. I know you want to take care of this, but its already taken care of so there's no need. Stop adding extra stress to yourself when you don't have to."

"You're right." He nodded like he finally had clarity on things, but Anastasia knew he probably still wanted Zyree dead.

"So, now that that's out of the way, how do you feel about moving to Atlanta?" she asked with her brows raised. He whipped his head around to face her and shrugged.

"We was just talkin bout that shit earlier," he mused. "I don't think it's a bad idea actually. You get to be close to your sisters, I get to be closer to my brother, and it's great for business, but I thought you loved the new house."

"It's alright, but I love you and my family more," she told him as she snuggled closer.

"Well, Atlanta it is then," he said. Anastasia wasn't really surprised that he agreed. Like he said it was a win win. Now, all she had to do was figure out if she would work with Lexi at the club. They'd never worked together before, and she was sure it would be just as wild as their lives were being together so much, especially with Lexi as their boss, but it wouldn't be them if it wasn't some drama involved. As bad as she wanted to jump up and call her sisters to tell them right then, D'Mani kissing on her neck had her stuck in place with other things on her mind. She'd tell them the next day when they got together that she was moving to Atlanta and accepting the job.

Chapter 31

The sounds of *Rock With You* by the one and only Michael Jackson filled the kitchen as the Holiday Sisters whipped up breakfast. Victoria had tried to come in and help, but it was easy to throw the babies off on her to keep her away. It was funny how times had changed. Before Abraham died, you couldn't get Victoria out of Mississippi, but she left every chance she got lately and had damn near moved without making it official. Her, along with Aunt Shirley spent time between Drea and Lexi's houses and surprisingly everything was going smooth.

"Lexi, don't burn the bacon," Lyssa fretted.

"Bitch, you always got sum to say wit yo outta work ass. Your new hire packet is still on my desk so you better chill out," Lexi snapped.

"This bitch. See Drea this is all…"

"Sisteerrrssss… it's the weekend. We've all been getting along fine and let's leave work at work please," Drea cut Lyssa off.

All of the sisters looked at her like she was crazy and then erupted into laughter.

"How the fuck we gon leave work at work and all of our asses work together?" Lexi finally said.

"Y'all make me sick," Drea rolled her eyes as she finished up the pancakes.

Anastasia was finishing up the fruit tray and Alyssa was pouring Mimosas when Aunt Shirley walked in.

"Less juice and more champagne in mine… you know what, just move so I can make my own." She bumped Lyssa out of the way.

"Aunt Shirley, I'ma…"

"You gon what?" Lexi chimed in.

"Beat both of y'all asses," Lyssa replied and Stasia stepped by her side.

Both Lexi and Aunt Shirley laughed in their faces.

"Calm down, Craig… you know we just playing but don't write a check ya ass can't cash."

"Shirley, who you in here bothering?" Victoria walked in and asked with Ava in her arms.

"Let's put the food out and eat y'all… everything is done," Drea chirped.

She grabbed the platter of pancakes and looked at the time on the stove and noticed that it was a little after ten. They had been in the kitchen since about 8:30 cooking and clowning around. After placing the tray that she had down, she went to D'Mari's man cave and opened the door. She knocked a couple of times and then twisted the knob, only to find it locked. A few seconds later, the door opened and there stood Mari with a stupid grin on his face.

"Why y'all got the door locked?"

"We didn't want any of y'all to bust in on us, baby… we talking business."

She looked past him and surveyed the room. D'Mani, Corey, and J.R. all looked like they were up to no good, but she shrugged it off.

"Breakfast is ready," she told him and left.

Mari spanked her on the ass as she walked off and she turned around and smiled at him.

"Don't start no shit."

"You know I can finish it." He smirked.

Before she made it back to the kitchen, she heard DJ making baby talk on the monitor. He didn't wake up crying a lot, that was left to Ava. She made her way to him and he began smiling as soon as he saw her face. After checking his diaper and seeing that he was wet, Drea changed her baby and then made her way back to the family. Everyone was getting settled and ready to eat. Drea noticed that the guys had gotten extremely close. That could be good, but it could also be bad. She shook herself out of lawyer mode and sat down beside her husband. Victoria blessed the food and they all dug in. Lyssa passed the Mimosa's around and Drea contemplated taking a drink. She hadn't consumed any liquor since finding out that she was pregnant, but she knew that her turn up time was near. The Holiday Sisters were going out later that night and Lexi's grand opening was on Labor Day. Drea noticed that Lexi poured some orange juice instead of drinking out of the glass Lyssa gave her and knew that was strange. Once again, she pushed her thoughts to the side and dug into her food.

Later that night, the guys left and went in one direction and the girls went in another. Drea was driving with Lexi riding shot gun and Lyssa and Stasia holding it down in the back. They knew that Aunt Shirley was going to cuss them all out for sneaking out and leaving her, but the night was all about the sisters and she could celebrate with them on Monday. Lexi was in control of the music and Drea had no idea what the hell she was playing. She was so out of the loop, but she knew that after a few drinks she would be just fine.

"Wait... why didn't we Uber? Who gon be the designated driver?" Drea turned the music down and asked.

"I'll drive us back, hoe... you have a good time tonight," Lexi told her.

"Well, I was gonna say Lyssa's pregnant ass can drive, but Lexi got it," Stasia chimed in.

"Damn, why I keep forgetting yo ass pregnant. My bad. But you ain't drinking Lexi?" Drea looked at Lyssa in the mirror and then turned to Lexi.

"I be forgetting that bitch pregnant, too. She got it," Lexi said and turned the music back up.

"It still seems surreal honestly. My ass woulda got there and tried to drink, too," Lyssa said.

Drea was about to say something else to Lexi, but she changed her mind as she made the turn on Ponce De Leon Avenue. A few minutes later, she turned into the parking lot of Boogalou Restaurant and Lounge. They all agreed not to go to a 'club club', and J.R. recommended that place. The parking lot was packed and Drea hoped that they would be able to get a table. Each of the sisters gathered their clutches, made sure they looked good and exited the vehicle. Drea admired her sisters and if she had to say so herself, they were some fine ass women and the men they had were blessed to have them.

As soon as they stepped inside, Drea knew that they were about to have a great night. The music was on point and everyone seemed to be having a good ass time, from some people sitting down eating, to others up dancing. They were escorted to a booth and they sat down and got comfortable. Without wasting anytime, Drea ordered six shots of Patron, three for each of them, excluding Lyssa of course. Lexi grabbed the menu and ordered some chicken wings, a pizza and a Dr. Pepper, so the everyone else followed suit and ordered some food after she made it clear that she wasn't sharing. When the waitress brought the shots back, Drea picked one up and toasted to her first real night out since giving birth and her first drink in almost ten damn months.

Drea threw her shot back and put the glass back down. She looked and noticed that four glasses were still full instead of three.

"Lexi, you got me hooked on your favorite drink and you acting lame… why?" Drea quizzed.

"I wanna eat first, Drea, damn!"

"When you started caring about eating before you drink?" Stasia asked.

"If you bitches don't leave me alone… I got this," Lexi fussed.

Drea had an idea of why Lexi's ass wasn't drinking, but she would wait to get her alone before saying anything. She knew how stubborn and feisty her baby sister was. She wasn't about to beg her to drink, instead she picked up two of the glasses and downed the shots back to back.

"Drea, you better slow down… it's been a minute since you had alcohol," Lyssa warned her.

"I got this, sis," Drea said and ordered another round.

***

The next morning, Drea woke up and hopped out of the bed. Nothing looked familiar and she wondered where the fuck she was. Before she could try to figure it out, she rushed to the door and prayed that it was the bathroom, and it was. She reached the toilet just in time. Her head was pounding and Drea felt like shit.

"I bet you'll eat before you drink next time," Lexi appeared and handed Drea a towel.

"What the fuck happened and where we at?"

"We at my house. Bitch, your husband woulda left yo ass if he woulda saw you last night." Lexi laughed.

"I don't remember shit," Drea admitted.

"Oh, don't worry… I got videos."

"And I do, too." Lyssa appeared.

"Fuck y'all… let me get myself together so I can get home to my babies."

"Naw, look at these videos first." Lexi handed her the phone.

Drea couldn't believe what she was seeing. She had definitely made up for lost time the night before.

"I'm not drinking again," she confessed.

"You a lie. My grand opening tomorrow," Lexi reminded her.

"Oh yeah, you right, but I'll be sure to eat first." Drea laughed and that made her head hurt worse.

"Be like me next time." Lexi rolled her eyes.

"That might be a good idea… or not." She side eyed Lexi who looked away and told them to come and eat breakfast.

Drea didn't put up a fuss because she needed to put something on her stomach, but she couldn't wait to get Lexi alone so that they could talk. It was true that all of the sisters

were closer than ever, but some shit would just never change.

Chapter 32

"I'm so nervous that I gotta throw upppppppppp!"

Lexi ran to the bathroom just in time to empty the bacon and eggs she ate that morning into the sink.

"Alexis, pull it together, bitch," Marcus yelled from the bedroom in her condo.

"I'm sorry, I can't help it," she yelled back, before grabbing her toothbrush off of the sink's counter.

After she was done brushing, she took the Colgate mouthwash and splashed it around in her mouth before grabbing a towel and cleaning her face off. Once she completed those tasks. She joined Marcus back in the room at the same the doorbell rang.

"Those my sisters. Grab that for me while I throw my shoes on," she requested, reaching on the top shelf of her closet and grabbing a Giuseppe shoe box.

Lexi sat on the bed and pulled out a pair of open toe spiked heel shoes. She had ordered those shoes especially for the day and knowing her, she might not wear them again after today.

"SEXI LEXI, YOU READY?" Drea yelled as soon as she walked through the doors of her bedroom.

"Damn, why you looking so ugly?" Stasia stopped in the doorway and asked, noticing the grimace look on her sister's face.

"Yeah, Baby Holiday, what's wrong?" Lyssa quizzed, taking a seat on the bed next to her.

"I'm just nervous y'all. What if everything fails? What if motherfuckers not feeling my club?" she whined.

"Girl, shut up. Damn near everybody in the A knows you. You always the life of the party, who wouldn't want to come and fuck with you?" Stasia replied, making Lexi feel a little better.

"You right, maybe I'm overthinking. Let's go!"

Lexi stood to her feet and walked over to the full-length mirror, giving herself a final look over. She wore a pair of all-white Gucci high waist pants that fit her like a glove. An all-white Gucci crop top, with a gold linked Gucci belt hanging from her waist. The all white Giuseppe shoes completed her look.

"You fine, bitch; now let's slide. Shirley's ass waiting in the car," Lyssa said, standing to her feet.

"Why she ain't come up?"

"Girl, she been talking to her man the whole ride over here," Drea stated.

"They ass probably having phone sex while y'all up here," Lexi laughed.

"Ugggghhhh my seats!" Drea yelled, running out the door and to her truck.

"Too late, Aunt Shirley's nasty ass juices all over them bitches," Marcus yelled out to her, causing everyone to laugh.

Once Lexi put a coat of lip gloss on her lips and grabbed her Gucci clutch, they all headed out the door in their all-white attire. Marcus, Aunt Shirley and Lexi, got inside of Marcus's car while the other Holiday sisters lead the way in Drea's ride. As soon as they secured themselves in their seatbelt, Lexi reached inside her bag and pulled out an already rolled blunt and handed it to Shirley who was chilling in the backseat.

"Don't mind if I do." She smirked, grabbing it from Lexi's hand and sparking it up.

After a few hits, she handed it back to Lexi who passed it to Marcus. Marcus took one hit and passed it to Lexi who declined.

"You ok?" Aunt Shirley reached her arm around to the front seat and felt Lexi's forehead.

"Girl, I'm good." She giggled, swatting her hand away.

"I just need to stay focused and that weed from Bankhead is some dangerous shit," she explained.

"Whatever, more weed for me," Shirley replied, hitting the blunt and almost coughing up a lung.

The ride to HS4 was a little under an hour. Lexi's nerves had calmed down a bit but as soon as she pulled up and seen those flashing lights, she felt like she was about to shit bricks.

"Best friend, look at this shit; it's all you, baby," Marcus beamed as he parked in front of the club.

A surreal feeling took over the nerves that once controlled Alexis's body. Words couldn't describe how she was feeling. She wished her father was there to see his baby girl open her first business but she knew he was looking down smiling. She planned on taking plenty of pictures to show her mom who was watching the twins and Kyler.

"HOLIDAY SISTER BITCHESSSSS!" Anastasia yelled as she walked up the street with Drea and Lyssa in tow.

"This shit so dope, I'm so proud if you," Lyssa said, hugging Lexi before the other sisters joined in, making it a group hug.

Once their embrace was over, Jen, one of J.R.'s workers pulled Lexi to the red carpet so the photoshoot could begin. After snapping a few pictures, she grabbed her sisters and took a couple with them before doing the same with Marcus and Aunt Shirley.

"Can somebody go get J.R.?" Lexi requested and within minutes, he was hugging her from behind as they smiled for the cameras.

"Turning your grand opening to an all-white Labor Day party was genius, bae," J.R. said, smacking her on the ass as they made their way through the double metal doors and into her establishment.

The club was lit already and Lexi was loving it. Half naked women with bodies to die for, hung from the ceilings, while some of the best dancers shook their ass on the stage. The servers made sure that drinks flowed effortlessly while the DJ kept the hits coming back to back.

"I'm finna mingle a bit, I'll be back," Lexi told J.R. and her family who headed to the VIP section.

Lexi did just as she promised, she mingled with the people she knew as well as strangers. She was humble and wanted to thank everyone for coming out to support her. It was easy to see that everyone was having a good time just by the way the club was turned up. After making a few new friends, Lexi headed back over to where her family and closest friends were. D'Mani, Corey and D'Mari had finally arrived and was taking shots with the crew.

"The woman of the hour is here!" D'Mari yelled, raising his shot glass in the air.

"Toast. Toast. Toast," they all chanted as they passed the Patron around and poured some in their glasses.

Lexi smiled like a kid on Christmas morning as she embraced all the love. She wanted this feeling to last forever.

"Here!" Corey said, handing Lexi a glass.

"Nah, I'm good. I gotta stay focused." she replied, grabbing a bottle of water off the table while her sisters eyed her suspiciously.

Lexi shrugged off their stares before dancing a little. Her and the family danced four songs straight until her two-thousand-dollar shoes began to get the best of her.

"Bae, I got some flip flops in my office, come with me to get them," she requested, pulling at J.R.'s hand who followed behind her without putting up a fuss.

They were able to dip through the crowd without running into anyone. Once inside her office, she closed the door and stepped out of her shoes.

"You good, bae?" J.R. asked, taking a seat on the edge of her desk.

"I am but I wanted to get you alone to give you something." She smiled, as she walked over towards him.

"Straight up." he replied, licking his lips.

Lexi planted herself between his legs before sneaking a kiss.

"I know your birthday isn't until tomorrow but I got your gift now," she gushed.

"Baby, I told you that you didn't have to give me anything." he replied.

"I know. I know but this is something that you really wanted."

Lexi moved from between his legs and walked over to her purse that was on her cherry Oakwood desk. She went inside and pulled out a long jewelry box

"Here, open it." She giggled.

J.R. eyed her briefly before following her instructions. Once he took the top off, his eyes widen and a smile bigger than the Grinch's invaded his face.

"ARE YOU FUCKING SERIOUS!" he yelled, bass filling his voice as Lexi shook her head up and down.

"BABY IS THIS SHIT REAL?" he questioned, still filled with excitement.

"Yes baby, you are going to be a daddy." She grinned before falling into his arms.

J.R. stared at the pregnancy test and just smiled before hugging Lexi. He lifted her off her feet and spun her around in the air.

"Aw shit my bad, probably making my lil nigga dizzy. Sorry son." He kneeled down to her flat stomach and apologized.

"Let's go tell everybody." Lexi laughed before heading back out to the crowd.

Once they were back in their section, J.R. ordered everyone a round of drinks, causing them to wonder why he was in such a good mood all of a sudden.

"Aye look y'all! I wanna toss this bitch back for my wife. She's a brand-new club and soon to be a brand-new mother." J.R. yelled over the music.

"BITCH, WE KNEW IT!" the Holiday sisters yelled out in unison before jumping to their feet and hugging Lexi.

"When did this happen?" Drea asked.

"Well, this one time, at yo crib…. We fucked in yo bathroom," Lexi blurted out.

"You a dirty hoe." Drea laughed, kissing her little sister on the jaw.

The crew partied until they couldn't party anymore. The DJ began to wind down by two that morning and the club was cleared out by three.

"It's officially your birthday. Happy Birthday, Daddy" Lexi smiled as she snugged up close to J.R. while he locked things up.

"Thank you, mommy," he replied, locking the doors.

Everyone walked to their respectful cars, all the women with shoes in hand. The guys made sure the women were safe and secured before they wrapped up whatever conversation they were having. Lexi stared out the window at J.R. as they congratulated him again. Her heart smiled, she had finally found someone to make her feel complete and the baby in her stomach, may just be what it takes to slow Sexi Lexi down. Who knows, maybe or maybe not.

"Bitch, you finally trapped my man, huh?" Aunt Shirley said from the backseat.

"Girl, go to sleep." Lexi laughed.

Within literally a matter of sixty seconds, loud snores came from behind her. Lexi wanted to tell her to shut up but instead, she went to her Facebook app and posted a picture of her and J.R., wishing him a happy birthday. Lexi glanced out of the rearview mirror, the sound of tires screeching alerted her. She looked up just in time to see a black Nissan Altima flying down the street. She watched as the passenger side and back window rolled down and two hand guns appeared, aimed at the Holiday sister's men. Completely frozen, Lexi did the only thing she could do and that was yell out to J.R. but it was a little too late, the sounds of gunfire, echoed through the air.

FIND OUT WHAT HAPPENS NEXT IN "THE ROC BOYZ: MONEY, POWER AND RESPECT" YES, YOU GET THE BOYZ STORY!! COMING DECEMBER 1ST!!!

Sweet September!!

Read all Cole Hart Signature Releases for the month of September to be entered into the drawing!!

Each book will have the next release at the end, along with a time frame to answer each question or send a code!!

Question 1

What did Andrea and D'Mari name the twins?

Email Answers to:

colehartcash@yahoo.com

***ALL ANSWERS ARE DUE BY (SEPTEMBER 2, 2018 AT 11:59 PM). THE WINNER(s) WILL BE ANNOUNCED IN COLE HART SIGNATURE READERS CLUB ON OCTOBER 1st ***

RELEASING

SEPTEMBER 3, 2018

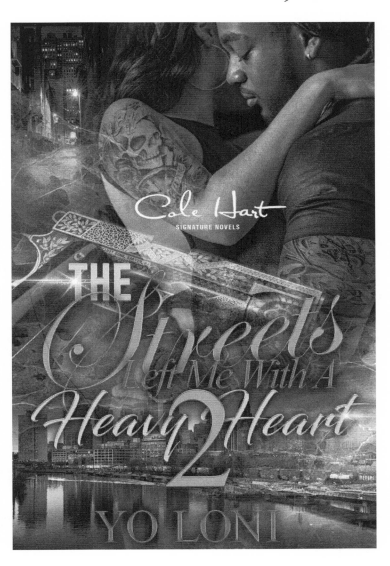

Made in the USA
Middletown, DE
10 February 2022

60940557R00194